PRAISE FOR
DAVID ALBAHARI

"Between adventure and apocalypse . . . Kafka and
Kubrick . . . combining in grotesque-comical manner
all the ridiculousness, beauty, horror, subtlety and
extravagance that literature can hold."

NEUE ZÜRCHER ZEITUNG

"The book's single paragraph encourages reading it
in one sitting . . . . Even translated from his native
Serbian, Albahari's prose has the contemplative, tex-
tured quality of such Eastern European writers as
Kundera."

JOHN GREEN, *BOOKLIST*

"Albahari makes us feel how fiercely the present needs
to know the past. The present is an expression of the
past, whether we know what it was or we don't, and

when there exists only a void between us and our antecedents, he suggests, it is this void, rather than what ought to be our own lives, that will claim us. The book is a sophisticated meditation on the inextricability of historical memory and identity; it is also a gorgeous work of the imagination about an act of imagination. The tone is pure, as strange as can be, and hypnotizing."

DEBORAH EISENBERG, BOMB

"Albahari has written another investigation into the dark currents flowing just beneath the surface of human experience, and we should feel lucky to follow him down."

JESSA CRISPIN, NPR BOOKS

"Albahari is one of the great writers of this world and we do not know it, or not enough."

LA VIE LITTÉRAIRE

CHECKPOINT

ALSO BY DAVID ALBAHARI

DAVID ALBAHARI

CHECKPOINT
A NOVEL

Translated from the Serbian by
Ellen Elias-Bursać

RESTLESS BOOKS
BROOKLYN, NEW YORK

Copyright © 2010, 2018 David Albahari
Translation copyright © 2018 Ellen Elias-Bursać

First published as *Kontrolni Punkt*
by Stubovi kulture, Belgrade, 2010

First Restless Books paperback edition September 2018

Paperback ISBN: 9781632061928
Library of Congress Control Number: 2018938301

Cover design by Matt Dorfman
Set in Garibaldi by Tetragon, London

Printed in Canada

1 3 5 7 9 10 8 6 4 2

Restless Books, Inc.
232 3rd Street, Suite A111
Brooklyn, NY 11215

restlessbooks.org
publisher@restlessbooks.org

CHECKPOINT

FROM WHERE WE STOOD, the logic of setting up a checkpoint on this particular spot was clear—this was the highest point on a road that rose and fell just as steeply up to and away from the barrier and sentry box. Though we never actually measured it, the stretch of road leading uphill was the same in length as the stretch running down. If somebody were to walk from one side, from below, from exactly where the slope began, while somebody else was walking up from the other side at the same time—assuming, of course, that all the elements of their stride were equal and they were moving at the same pace—the two would reach the barrier at the exact same moment. In fact, each would arrive simultaneously at their side of the barrier, and from there they'd stare *beyond* the barrier at the other. On their way back, assuming the same conditions, of course, the same would occur. In other words, both would reach the level part of the road that extended in front of them and disappeared off into the forest. We never spent time in the forest, not because we'd been told not to but because we were all from the city so the forest meant nothing to us. Had one of us gone into the forest, he probably never would have reappeared, the only exception being Mladen, who'd lived on a mountainside. The forest for him was home sweet home, and it may be that our whole platoon was assigned the task of guarding the barrier and checkpoint because of Mladen's knowledge of forest flora. Apparently, he'd given the right answer to the question about what soldiers should eat if they're forced to hunker down in the wild. So that's how we ended up here, at least for now, and after the first week it's looking as if we won't be reassigned any time soon. This was a conclusion we came to on our own because during that first week no one showed up at either side of the barrier, and the radio that was supposed to connect us to the command center fell silent the second day after we arrived and would later kick in now and then only at the odd moment. The soldiers didn't dare carry cell phones because of their interference with the military network, and none of the three phones the unit had were working as there was no electric power available for recharging. So, having no contact with headquarters or the world, we could be said to be as lost as castaways surrounded by a boundless expanse of ocean. Worst of all, we had no way of knowing which route we'd taken to get there. The trucks that brought us drove through the night and unloaded us before dawn on the broad path leading through the forest all the way to the checkpoint, and then immediately, while everything around us was still dark, they turned around and back they went. When dawn finally broke, no one was sure which road the trucks had used. All around us were tire tracks, of course, but they crisscrossed and overlapped every which way so we couldn't identify the road leading back to home base. But we only began to wonder about this a few days later once the unusual quiet of the place had begun to stir our qualms, by which time the tire tracks were barely visible, especially on the grass that had straightened since then. We had no choice but to continue doing what we'd come there to do: guard and watch over the passing of people and goods through the checkpoint. To be honest, we hadn't even been told whether the checkpoint was on a border lying between two countries or along a line dividing two villages. Perhaps it didn't matter. A soldier's duty, after all, is not to reason why, his is but to obey and only then ask questions—meaning, if we'd been told to guard the checkpoint, that's what we'd do, and we wouldn't distract ourselves with idle guesswork. So our commander promptly drew up a roster of sentries, cutting back on the number of daytime sentries so the soldiers would be more rested at night, when, for security reasons, there were four on duty. Nothing moved around us by day or night—all the sentries concurred, but our commander, an old-school soldier, had no intention of relenting or reducing the number of sentries on night duty. "Where nothing squeaks," our commander said, "that's where the trouble is brewing." So we guarded a checkpoint where nobody was checked and peered through our binoculars at landscapes through which no one passed. If there was a war still on somewhere, we knew nothing about it. No shots were fired, there was no zinging of bullets, no bomb blasts, no helicopter clatter, nothing. "What if the war's already over," we asked our commander one morning, "shouldn't we be going home?" He was implacable. "We'll go home when they send us home. Until then, here we stay." The soldiers protested, stood there, cried, "Release us, send us home!" The commander did what he could to quiet them but without success. A fractious mob is a fractious mob, whether they're soldiers or civilians. No one listened to the commander, so, in the end, he had to resort to an unappealing but tried-and-true remedy: the pistol. Raising it high above his head, he barked that he'd start shooting if they didn't all shut up and return to their posts. A shot was heard. The commander stared, aghast, at his pistol; but the shot hadn't come from him. It had come from the gun of one of the sentries who, after we'd assembled by the checkpoint, reported to the commander in a quavering voice that he'd shot when he thought a man in green fatigues had shot at him first. "This is not a thinking matter," barked the commander. "Did he or did he not shoot at you?" "He took aim," said the guard, "but I was faster." The commander sent a group of soldiers to examine the place where the person in the green fatigues had supposedly stood, and they ran off across the meadow. Someone said maybe a bear had devoured a woodsman earlier, and everyone burst out laughing. A little later the group of scouts waded back through the brambles. They were holding something green, which turned out to be a tatter of ragged fatigues. Nowhere, however, said the scouts, did they find anything to suggest that this filthy, rumpled tatter was what the sentry had seen. Nowhere, they insisted, was there any trace of humans, nothing but paw prints and bird tracks. Did this mean the sentry hadn't seen anything? The commander said nothing. Then he announced the alarm was over and called an assembly. We lined up and, while the sun warmed our heads from behind, we listened to the commander's warning to remain calm if we wished to grapple with the enemy. True, we knew nothing of who the enemy might be, but once a war is on one speedily acquires both friends and foes. Back we went to our duties—at least those of us who had duties—and our leisure activities, and soon the strains of an accordion could be heard. The cook's helpers brought news of the goulash we'd be served for dinner and there were rumors that there might be cake, which sparked elation among the soldiers and helped them forget how horrific our situation was. But then the horror showed its ugly face with the commander's order that over the next few days, or rather, nights, we were to use lights only in cases of the most dire need, and all evening activities such as polishing boots, cleaning weapons, and longer stays outdoors would be reduced to a minimum or switched to daytime. Then smoking came up, which had not been permitted in enclosed areas but only at a distance of ten feet from the building where the men were billeted. We should explain that the checkpoint was not new, nor were the barracks where we were housed, with sleeping quarters, a lecture hall, a bathroom, a mess hall, and a small room for the commander. There were also two latrines near the barracks dating back to whenever, slapped together from unpainted boards and thick with flies and spiders. In one of them, the next morning, a murdered sentry was found. The ones who saw him said he was sitting there, his pants down around his ankles, with a nasty gash across his neck. His gun was propped in the corner, and everything was drenched in blood. When he saw him, the commander cursed with a gasp, spun on his heel, and returned to his office. We stayed outside and spoke in whispers. The sun climbed higher in the sky, and the day warmed. Clouds of flies swarmed around the latrine. They hung in the air like clusters of grapes, and soon the sentry's entire body had begun to look more like a blackened mummy. The commander finally came out, and when he addressed us we could smell the drink on him. He set two men to digging a grave, then other soldiers joined in and soon the grave was ready. "The priest," said the commander, "where's our priest?" He was referring to a soldier who, after three years as a seminary student had transferred to the school of natural sciences and mathematics to study physics and chemistry. The commander dispatched four soldiers to fetch the dead body, and soon they returned, toting it on the door they'd pulled off the latrine hinges, and behind them swarmed and quivered the clouds of flies. "Quick," said the commander. "Make it quick." The "priest" began mumbling and chanting, the murdered sentry was rolled into the grave, the military-issue shovels scooped in the dirt, and, in the time it took to clap two hands together, a mound of black and greasy soil piled up before us. Only later did someone think to poke an improvised cross into it, but we never learned who. Nor did we find out who killed him, because after the first rumors of some sort of forest avengers lurking in treetops and waiting for us to drop off to sleep before creeping in and murdering someone, a question arose, which nobody uttered aloud, but which struck all of us as a genuine possibility: what should we do if it was one of us who'd done him in? We don't know who first thought of the question, but afterwards it could easily be seen traveling from soldier to soldier, always scribbling the same astonishment on their faces. In the evening the soldiers tossed and turned for hours, sleepless, chilled by the thought that if the killer were already in their midst they might be next on the list. They dropped off to sleep in the most varied postures, on the floor by their cot, with elbows on the windowsill, or by the front door—a cigarette between fingers, until, in the end, the commander flew into a rage and said he'd ban all smoking. And even if he hadn't blustered as he did, smoking was on its way out. Whoever still had a pack tucked away hid it like a snake hides its legs; as there was no opportunity to stockpile tobacco, the same fate awaited them all. It's easy to imagine that this worry was what pushed the men to talk among themselves about how to make their way back through the forest. We won't just sit here, will we, waiting for someone to stab us, one by one, in the back? They called for the commander to do something, and, after conferring with his officers, he ordered the formation of two squads of scouts. The squads were identical, three men each; one (in each squad) carried a light machine gun, while the others were armed with lighter weapons and hand grenades. The squad leaders were also issued flare guns; what with the total lack of all communications this would be their only way of signaling their location if they were in crisis. The commander wanted at first to assign Mladen to one of the squads, and the soldiers themselves assumed he would, but then the thinking prevailed that Mladen should be reserved in case there was a search for one or both of the scouting parties. And so it was that the next day at dawn both squads lined up by the checkpoint barrier, one on one side, the other on the other, heard what the commander had to say, saluted, and marched off down the hill. As we've already said, the distance from the checkpoint to the foot of the hill was almost identical on both stretches of the road, and the groups reached the points where the road curved off into the forest at nearly the same moment. Once they were all out of sight, a hush settled over those of us who still stood around the checkpoint. The first to speak was the commander, who asked what there was for dinner, though he knew the answer every bit as well as all the rest of us: mac and cheese, beet salad, and a large chocolate-chip cookie. This was when someone thought to ask whatever had happened to the tattered scrap of fatigues found in the bushes, did anyone know? "Yes," said the commander, "of course, we examined the uniform, or, I should say 'the scrap,' since somebody had ripped the uniform to shreds." This was followed by a thorough disquisition on how many scraps there had been, the force required for ripping them, and, ultimately, how there was nothing left to suggest where the uniform had been manufactured and obtained or who had worn it. The only item available to shed some light, though a feeble light rather than a strong one, was a tarnished token with the number 5 pressed into both sides. "Such tokens," explained the commander, "are usually used for public telephones or metro rides, but there are no insignia to suggest which city or state uses such a token. And perhaps it's no longer in use," continued the commander. "It may be a vestige of some long-gone time, a memento, perhaps, that its former owner held on to for years and then forgot in the back pocket of his discarded fatigues. Who knows, he may be searching for it anxiously as we speak, rifling through everything he owns in vain." The soldiers' faces fell and they patted their pockets where they, apparently, carried similar mementos. One soldier asked to inspect the token, and it quickly traveled from hand to hand, but no one could say anything about it. There were several arbitrary guesses that don't merit mention. Better, now, a word about the strength of the forces assigned to guard the checkpoint. We've said nothing about this so far, and later there may not be time. So, under him the commander had a cook and a nurse, and three ten-man units, each with a junior officer as leader. The nurse also served as clerk, quartermaster, radio and telegraph operator, and probably even more. No longer, however, could we speak of three ten-man units; the murder of the sentry in the latrine meant there were two fully manned units and one only partially manned. Perhaps the word "murder" was not the best, as there had been no official statement yet as to cause of death. A few wanted to call the murder a suicide; to do so would relieve the army of responsibility, but in this case that would have been ludicrous. The gash on the right side of his neck could never have been inflicted by the sentry himself, especially as he was right-handed. A suicide would have been easier on the rest of us; there'd have been no need for special caution when we used the latrine. But knowing someone had ambushed him while he was in there groaning and straining to expel his waste, the soldiers began going to the latrine in pairs, sometimes even in a gang of five or six. And while one of them sat inside, the other or others would stand guard. Night, however, posed a problem: no one dared venture out to the latrine in the dark, so we prepared a small room to serve as a nighttime toilet. The two, three buckets were carried out as soon as we woke, emptied, and cleaned for the next night. Fortunately, the soldiers were mainly young men, and there weren't many who had to slink off to the buckets at night, but nevertheless all soldiers were assigned to the duty of hauling them out and emptying them—not a task they enjoyed, but if everybody could be happy all the time there'd be no army, right? The commander was unbending and ready to punish anyone who disrupted the order; he was right there, the next morning, to carry out the first bucket, sloshing with urine and excrement, and dump it down the latrine. In the evening, when the daily orders for the next day were read out, he'd announce who was on "sanitation" duty for the next morning, and they were dubbed "shitty granny" or "shitty gramps" by the soldiers. But these nocturnal forays remind us that we need to explain how we managed once night fell. First, we had a few kerosene lamps, standard issue for rustic bivouacs, places where there'd probably be only intermittent electric current and other power, and beyond that every soldier was issued a package of slow-burning candles, and there were also plenty of extra candles in the squad depot. Kerosene lamps and big candles, flames in the night air, created a romantic mood and who knows what someone might have thought when seeing so many flames flickering in the dark barracks. More eyes might have been watching than we knew. Hence the difference between us and "them": they always knew more about us than we about them, especially when it came to numbers. Whatever the case, the next morning we found a dead raven. One of its legs had been crushed, its wings snapped, its beak plucked out. The soldiers pressed around it, shouted and cursed. They were more unsettled by the dead bird than by the latrine sentry murder. "Whoever they are, they're not human," said one soldier, "they're monsters and they deserve to die!" "Now!" shouted other soldiers and gathered around the commander when he came over to see what was up. They pointed to the raven, but apparently the commander was not as alarmed; he told them to pull themselves together. "Our men are out in the forest," said the commander, "and until they return, no one moves, understand?" The soldiers mumbled something conciliatory and returned to their duties. The sun beat down merci-lessly, most unusual for the time of year, and some of the soldiers quickly tanned to a bronze, but there were others whose backs, arms, and shoulders, and, I should add, faces became a mass of blisters. "We won't be sleeping tonight," thought the commander, but then the cry went up: "Here they are, they're coming!" When the commander ran over to the checkpoint there they were: the squads had apparently each lost a man. In each, the two surviving soldiers were carrying a third. They toiled up the hillside and we, while they were still far away, could hear their labored breathing and choked coughs. Each squad reached the barrier at almost exactly the same moment, and someone remarked that somehow, somewhere in the forest, each must have taken a wrong turn: each returned to the same side of the checkpoint from which they'd left. But when the men were told, they insisted doggedly that they could not remember one path intersecting another nor that they were ever in doubt about which way to go. "The forest was hushed," said one of the soldiers, "and we took care to honor the quiet. Had we run into the other squad, our conversation would have sent out shockwaves like a bomb blast." This may explain why both soldiers were killed by arrows, an old-fashioned yet deadly weapon, the fletching still protruding from their chests. The commander fumed and swore up a storm, using curses even the worst drunks and bastards would have been proud of, though, obviously, nobody could blame him. Everything might have been different had we known why we were there, what we were protecting, from whom. What could possibly have been the point of a checkpoint on a road that no one ever traveled, which may have run in a circle? Or was its sole goal an illusion of passage, a chimera of progress, a launching pad for new victories, yet a trap, bait for the gullible, a carbon monoxide van to swallow souls, inside which people died from a surfeit—not a shortage—of air. Or, as one soldier put it, everything is so unreal precisely so that we won't figure out that "our side" was actually attacking us, unaware, perhaps, that we're "theirs." Who is "our side" in this war, anyway, where we're making this guest appearance, where even we have no idea what we're up to? Wouldn't it make more sense for us to march home and put this all behind us? "No, no, and no," scowled the commander. "There will be no homeward march. And besides," he asked, "where would we march to, and how—does anyone know? The telephone lines are down, the radios dead, we have no carrier pigeons to take our messages out, and even if someone were to set out for the headquarters, which road should they take to get there? Is there such a road?" The commander summoned the clerk and issued his order for the next day: we were to spend the whole day searching for a solution to our outlandish predicament. "We owe this to those who've died," announced the commander during our modest repast: a big roll and a small tin of sardines for each of us. During dinner something else happened, a story flew from ear to ear that men from one of the squads, only two of them, had caught sight of village dwellings in the distance through a haze across a clearing. One of them even swore he heard cows mooing and dogs barking. It was still early, wisps of fog swirled among the trees and over the meadows, but from the chimneys of the houses rose puffs of smoke, the household was up and about, probably at breakfast, and they'd soon be going out to tend to their morning duties. The soldiers, the two, even saw a front door slowly open, but then the order came to move on and off they went. They quickly told the squad leader, and he heard them out but wouldn't go back. That, he said, as the two soldiers reported, would give the advantage to whoever was following them, and there definitely were people, sad to say, who were out to ambush them without mercy. The commander heard the rumors and called the two men over. He asked the corporal who'd escorted them to step away because he didn't want any part of their conversation to leak out. He questioned the soldiers closely about the houses and farmyards they'd seen, and he even sketched a house in a few quick strokes to see if it resembled what they'd seen, despite or because of the fog, which had enticed them with its swirls. Once the soldiers had told him what they knew, the commander, as they later said, took from a drawer a map that had been folded and refolded many times, smoothed it out, placed a compass on the table, and gauged something for a time with the compass and a protractor. Of course, he might be mistaken, but if we gave him the benefit of the doubt, he said, then where those two soldiers said they'd seen houses and outbuildings, there was nothing, or, and now this really was strange, said the commander, there once had been houses like the ones they described, but—here he stopped and stared away into the distance—the whole area had been flooded a little farther north to make a reservoir for a hydroelectric dam that was never, said the commander, put into operation. Are you sure, he asked, now standing in front of the entire company, that the houses you saw weren't under water? But the soldiers were quick to dismiss this idea, and that what they'd seen might have been a mirage. Both laughed aloud as if they'd spent a whole evening practicing this in tandem. Someone said, "Let Mladen have a look," and they all hastened to concur. Mladen knew how to survive in the forest, so he'd know where to look and what to see. A spat later flared up about whether he should go alone or with an escort, but the commander interrupted this as it ended—or almost ended—saying we were out of time. A person alone is always more efficient than two or three. "In the old days," said the commander, "many an expedition floundered because the leader would have to keep track of an oversized crew: cooks, dog handlers, natives, masseuses." Then he suggested we ask Mladen whether he needed an escort. As far as he was concerned, said Mladen, an assistant might be helpful, but he was better off on his own. He'd be speedier and more effective, with no worries about what to do if his assistant were hit or, god forbid, killed, or, worse yet, captured and interned. "Well then," said the commander, "get ready and off you go. The sooner we know the truth about the houses and village, the sooner we can wrap this up." But a few soldiers noticed discrepancies between what the commander said before and his sudden tale of a power plant, and all this while waving the mysterious map. Where had it all come from is what the soldiers and others wanted to know. If he was commander, he couldn't be oblivious one minute, and then all talk the next as if he were a history expert. Then they all clammed up because Mladen appeared. Though nightfall was still hours away, he'd smeared his face with black paint; nothing gives a person away, he said, like moonlight shining on your face. Several soldiers came over to plead with him to take them along. Mladen urged them to go to the commander but they refused. One said he'd go with Mladen no matter what. "They'll shoot you between the eyes," said Mladen, pointing at the soldier's forehead and pulling an imaginary trigger. "I am, too, going," said the soldier, who raced off to pack, and no one ever saw him again. His disappearance was only noticed when Mladen came back to the checkpoint and asked what had happened to that pushy soldier who'd wanted to go with him no matter what. He'd thought of the man, said Mladen, when he sank into quicksand and tried to squirm free without losing his boots and weapons. He'd have given anything just then to have the young man along so he could reach out with a branch, but since the soldier wasn't there, Mladen struggled on his own. Luckily, he was mired in quicksand shallows, or whatever they're called, and bit by bit, inch by inch, he wriggled out onto solid, grassy turf. He lifted first one foot and then the other so we could see the mud caked to his boots. It took him only one night to reach the spot the two soldiers described, but he stayed there till daybreak to corroborate their story. Aha, said the commander, what did he see? He saw the house, like the soldiers said, but no smoke puffing from the chimney and the front door was not even open a crack. A window was open and curtains swayed in gusts of wind. He waited, said Mladen, till the sun climbed high in the sky but nobody appeared, not a soul stepped out of the house, not a farm animal left the barn; just when he thought it was time to return, he noticed a duck followed by an orderly trail of ducklings. The duck waddled over to the front door and Mladen could see it lift its beak; it was probably summoning someone, the person who, he assumed, regularly came out to feed them. "But the water?" asked the commander. "The water and the lake?" "No water, no lake," said Mladen. "Just carnage." The duck was quacking to someone and that persuaded him to venture out to see. No road led there, or he hadn't yet found it, so Mladen scrambled down a steep slope from the meadow, stepped across a gulch over a little brook, probably a seething torrent in the spring and summer rains, spilling over its narrow streambed. Hence the quicksand into which he'd so haplessly plunged. That's when he mentioned the soldier who'd wanted to tag along and only then did we realize the soldier was missing. The commander wrung his hands and sobbed with the breathy gasps of a woman, and then he pulled himself together and said he'd organize a rescue team and comb the terrain. "Absolutely not," said Mladen. "too late now, anyway. If he's alive, he's too far off to hear us, and if he's dead, all we can do is raise him a monument." "Forget it," called one of the soldiers. "Tell us what happened at the house!" First he came across a dog that had been gutted, Mladen told us, then he saw a cat with its spine broken, and in the barn he found two dead cows and a crazed horse. If animals were treated this way, wondered Mladen, what happened to the people? He thought it was time to go back, his assignment was only to see whether the houses did, in fact, exist, and not to find out what happened to the people who'd been living there. Then he heard moaning and forgot everything else. He hopped over a twisted fence, slowly approached the side of a building, and looked into the backyard. There he saw a ghastly scene: on a large wooden table lay two bodies: an older man, already dead, and an older woman, still alive and groaning in pain. Their bellies were slashed from side to side, partly disemboweled, their intestines dangling off the table. Mladen turned, he said, and when he went into the house he found the rest of the family: two young men, a woman, and a little girl. They had all, apparently, been raped and strangled or shot dead with a bullet to the head. Nothing in the house was touched, as if the marauders had taken care to be tidy. Judging by the few flies and no stench, Mladen figured the massacre must have happened the night before, and this made him especially cautious; he gave up looking further at other houses. And besides, he said, he didn't know whose side the victims were on, and who the murderers were fighting for. He'd called them murderers, he said, because if he were to call the people who'd perpetrated the atrocities by any other name, or referred to them as soldiers, he'd be insulting all those who'd respected treaties and conventions in wars. And nothing he'd seen hinted at who the perpetrators might be? asked the commander. The soldiers howled, saying they didn't even know whom they were up against. Maybe, said the soldiers, they were a buffer force sent to a conflict near their country's border, though maybe, said others, this is actually a civil war and they, as an official armed force, were dispassionately helping to subdue the conflicts. The commander stood, waited for the soldiers to quiet down, and then said he wished he could explain things to them, but he, too, was in the dark. "In the old days," he said, "this happened often; the kingdoms were vast and heralds had to travel for days to bring news to distant provinces of the end of a war. In the Second World War, on the little islands scattered across the Pacific, there were Japanese fighters who thought the war was still on for decades, and they'd shoot at every American who came near. Our situation is not as bad as all that," said the commander, "though our ignorance is appalling." But what could he do, he asked, when he was woken that night, as we were? He'd barely had time to pull on his uniform and rush downstairs to the jeep waiting for him out front. At the assembly point they'd said everything would be explained over the radio; the trucks were ready and required the cover of darkness. Well, sure, recalled the commander, he'd been handed an envelope with a map, the rosters of fighters, and lists of issued weapons and equipment. The lists were full of errors, said the commander, so he'd already made his own list of the things missing from the lists. The map was no good or out of date as we could see from Mladen's report and the stories of the soldiers who'd seen the house, where, according to the commander's map, there was supposed to be a reservoir. The commander looked like someone always on the verge of tears, but though we found this disturbing we didn't know how to help. Is the forest enchanted? mused someone. Is what we think to be happening nothing but an illusion? Who believes in magic? asked others, though no one could gainsay the possibility that hallucinogens had been used, but narcotics can't replace a magic wand, this we knew. Ever since our arrival, said the commander, he'd been doing nothing but juggling lists and making new ones. "It's all rife with errors," said the commander. "Not just the lists, the world. Wherever we go we'll find errors, most of all when they insist there aren't any." What he'd like, said the commander, was that there be no errors in the new roster he started yesterday, and he'd like that roster to stay brief, he sincerely hoped it would though he knew that no one, except just maybe He who was on high—here he stopped and raised his eyes to the heavens, and all of us looked upward after him—knows in advance just how long that roster will be. All of us, of course, understood what roster he had in mind, just as we all knew it held, so far, four names: the sentry killed in the latrine, the two men shot by arrows while patrolling the forest, and, finally, the soldier who set out on his own after Mladen. A hush. We were prepared to honor the victims of a war that, like every war, is pointless, but each of us was also hoping the next name wouldn't be his own. We said nothing and darted dirty looks at one another as if we were sworn enemies, but what else can you think of someone who hopes to see you dead? "I don't want to die," blurted one of us and we all burst out laughing, not that we were laughing at death, but with relief at the thought that all of us felt the same way. No one wanted to die. Even for such a noble cause as defending the homeland. What could possibly be noble about a violent death? And the stupidest part of all was that afterwards this would become fodder for people who'd had no experience at all with it, with death. How can a living person understand someone who's dead, understand what a gunshot victim thinks as the bullet rips through his flesh, understand the fever by which the organism races to close in and preserve its capacity to complete a last few actions that are built into the instinctual function of the human organism, especially regarding the proper dispatch of the soul into the cosmic strato-sphere? Yes, the soul launches like a rocket, but only those who are dispatched in a timely manner will arrive at their destination, while others, especially those rising from bodies that have fallen in the deprav-ity of a war, will continue to travel aimlessly through the transparent, gelid recesses of the cosmos, to throw themselves at the mercy of dissonant comets, crackpot satellites, meteors large and small, and other cosmic debris. Swathed in silken, diaphanous robes, the souls shiver softly, though during a war, whether global or local, a liberation or a conquest, long-standing obser-vation has registered an upsurge in the number of such souls, therefore rendering their shivering louder and more audible in the astronomical observatories where the sound is referred to as an astral hum. Science, of course, does not admit to the existence of souls, especially those shivering in the cosmic waste-lands, but that doesn't mean these souls aren't there and we shouldn't be doing all we can to protect them, just as we protect endangered animal species. Souls are in jeopardy, they're clobbered without mercy like baby seals, the difference being that the clobbering of baby seals is protested worldwide, while no one, nobody at all, stands up for those defenseless souls. But, enough, whoever's understood this gets it, and if they don't they probably never will. War, after all, is a godsend for nobody, don't forget this, because these words matter more than Heraclitus's stab at giving us war as the father of everything. And the mother? one asks. Where's she? Heraclitus has nothing to say about her, or maybe that particular fragment hasn't survived, or we've been misreading him. Whatever. There'll be no more repeating, and the commander will, regardless, keep a roster of the dead, murdered, or disappeared, and whoever wants to will be able to independently confirm the upside of having an efficient air-raid warning and broadcast system, then run to the nearest shelter, pull something over their head, and wait for all sounds to subside. The only thing still to be heard will be the shivering of the souls, like those harmonious sound curtains in performances of, say, Mike Oldfield or Soft Machine. Anyway, a soldier must think about death, and while the amateur fighter thinks about death in an amateur-ish way, the professional approaches it as a professional—death for the professional is no more than a clause in a contract. The amateur soldier, like all amateurs, generally speaks of things with pomposity, using long words and gnarly sentences. He might, for instance, say the "absorption of non-homogeneous phenomena, including the exploitation of the image of death as a universal, is a sufficiently grandiose conspiracy and, indeed, wellspring of alarm, which will most certainly amalgamate the negative charge of our every aspiration." And while the professional soldier merely shrugs at such platitudes, amateur fighters devote to them their best hours and days. They spew nonsense as if these are the ultimate mantras to elevate them high above the fray where the less fortunate wretches litter their lives like caramel candy wrappers. So much occurs to a person when faced with death, incredible! Of course, there are those who say that a summons to war is not a summons to death, that war is waged not for death but for life. We even heard the commander say, "War is life, not death." Okay, he whispered the words and never thought somebody might be listening, but so what. Words are words, whispered, shouted, or spat. Only when one is philosophizing do words perhaps cease to be words, though it's difficult to say just what they become once they aren't words. Instruments? Well, we'd come to guard the checkpoint and here we were fussing over words and philosophy. And not for a mere hour or two; days were passing in this philosophical haze and we wouldn't have been surprised, when we stepped outside, if we'd seen a yellow leaf and an apple and pear ripe for the picking. "Impossible," said the commander, and glanced at his watch, "we've only been here a week." "Longer," gasped the mob in a single voice, and the commander retreated. "Why provoke them," he said to himself, "when I can always find a way to outwit them?" A person might think everything was creaking and swaying in the unit like we were aboard a ship at sea, but he'd be so very wrong. We were a well-oiled unit and no one watching from the sidelines would ever think something was out of kilter. Even the next death didn't shake us, though it was no picnic to see one of the corporals hanging from the branch of a tree at the forest's edge. The first thought was suicide, but then we saw his hands tied behind his back, and a little later, in the bushes, somebody found the crate onto which the unfortunate corporal had probably been forced to climb only to have it kicked out from under him, and down he swung, his neck snapped, urine splashed down his legs. Meanwhile, for days the radio and telegraph operator had been attempting, in vain, to make contact with headquarters, and then one morning a woman's pleasant voice was picked up but in a different language. The radio and telegraph operator called the commander, who donned earphones and shut his eyes as if preparing to listen to a beloved opera; he listened for a few moments and then turned to the radio and telegraph operator and asked him if he had dialed a wrong number. The radio and telegraph operator said he hadn't been contacting headquarters over the phone lines, which anyone could listen in on, but that, at least until now, he'd made contact with headquarters over certain wavelengths that were supposedly secret. "If that's the case," said the commander, "headquarters has fallen to the enemy." But which enemy? was the question. What language was the person who'd answered speaking? asked the other soldiers and the radio and telegraph operator channeled the connection to the loudspeaker system. After crackling and hissing from the small speakers placed strategically around the whole area we were guarding, a voice reached us that was singing out words in a strange language. The commander promised a reward to anyone who could tell us what language this was, and there'd be no end to the rewards if they could translate for us what the person was actually saying. We sobered up and sharpened our ears. It was certainly not German or Russian, nor was it our language; then we eliminated English, Dutch, and French; it also wasn't Slovenian, Bulgarian, or Czech, nor was it Italian, Spanish, or Romanian, or Arabic, or Hebrew, or Chinese. "If we keep this up," piped a cheery voice, "we'll use up all the languages! And then what'll we do?" The commander warned the owner of this voice to watch his language because he could easily end up in the dock, and summary military courts are infamous for meting out the grimmest of sentences with cheer because any other approach might encourage insubordination. Then a soldier raised his hand, as if in school, waiting for his turn to speak, even holding up two fingers, the index and middle, so the teacher, or rather the commander, would call on him. "If this language sounds like so many others," said the soldier when the commander nodded in his direction, "might it be Esperanto?" Some applauded, others jeered, but most of them exchanged looks and shrugged. The soldier who'd asked the question couldn't have known that Esperanto had been the commander's great love when he was a child. How many days had he spent dreaming about a peaceful world, where everyone spoke the same language, as they had before the Tower of Babel! Esperanto seemed the most noble dream a human being might cherish. He considered saying a word or two to these army brats on the history of Esperanto and, of course, about the man who'd invented it, but he was afraid he might get carried away with the story and lured into an antiwar discourse, which would, he was certain, easily persuade the soldiers to accuse him of spreading pacifism and a negative attitude toward the armed forces, not only in our country but in general. At a moment when every chance for resistance should be glorified and patriotic ideas fundamentally encouraged, he, the commander, might be seen as a subversive, obliquely suggesting surrender. An anti-war discourse? I think not, concluded the commander, who would've been happiest sending this crew packing, but then he'd have found himself standing alone before a kangaroo court that would probably have no compassion for pacifists. But none of this helped with understanding what the person on the radio was saying; she continued, tirelessly, to prattle on in her wretched language. "Switch that off," said the commander, finally, and then, when silence reigned, he announced it was not Esperanto. Actually, what he said was: "This, sadly, is not Esperanto." They could think of him what they liked. He resisted the impulse to say something about a language meant to advance understanding among peoples, that the desire of the man who created this super-language had never waned, that today, maybe more than ever, there was a need for a language belonging to no one, meaning no ill will would be provoked just because this person or those people or the manager of some international concern was using the language. "Soldiers, sirs," he said finally, "we'll wait a little longer, a few more hours won't change a thing, and then we'll see what's what, especially if we haven't made contact with headquarters by then. In any case, we won't sit here wasting time, counting sheep." He'd only mentioned sheep symbolically, but he was astonished to see how many of the men turned to look for the sheep. They're inside you, thought the commander, inside you. For a moment he felt relief, but he knew this wouldn't last long so he strode off to his little room; two soldiers were already waiting there, one was Mladen, and the other, in fatigues, was someone the commander had never seen before. Later it transpired that he had seen the man but hadn't paid attention, just as he hadn't examined most of the soldiers carefully. They are, after all, thought the commander, merely consumer goods, cannon and tank fodder, and it is no good getting close to them; that plays havoc with the emotions, and if there is something a soldier, especially a professional soldier such as he, must never allow himself to foster and cultivate, that is emotions. Tearful eyes, a pounding heart, dry lips, and a swelling of the chest that is so difficult to describe, all these are things a soldier should respect but never indulge in. If your eyes tear up you'll see double, and if you take aim just then, who knows what you'll hit, and if your heart pounds at that very moment, your hand will tremble, and you won't be much use if the enemy attacks. The commander said all this without notes; he took pride in his way with words. He should've been a poet, thought the commander, and, resting his forehead on the windowpane, he gazed out at flowers in the meadow. Then he heard Mladen's discreet cough and his hand flew to his brow: how could he have forgotten the two soldiers. "Yes, Mladen," said the commander, and, turning to face them, found himself looking straight down the barrel of the other man's gun. "Bang," said the man, "bang-bang," and the commander could picture the bullet, spinning like a steel gyre, about to lodge itself in his heart. "We've come to negotiate," said Mladen. He started speaking and didn't stop for a long time, though two or three times he asked the other soldier to confirm or deny his words, which the soldier did with grace. All in all, the commander thought well enough of the soldier, mainly as a model for what all soldiers should be like, though he was none too thrilled by the ease with which the man kept him in his crosshairs. Even if by chance, thought the commander, especially if by chance. In short, Mladen said he'd been keeping a close eye on things since he arrived at the checkpoint, the mood among the soldiers was at its lowest ebb, unrest was on the rise, and at any moment he was expecting a revolt; a rebellion would have erupted already if the soldiers had had a clear sense of which road they could take and where to find "home." So, said Mladen, they'd sent a delegation to offer him, Mladen, a fee if he knew of or could find for them a path to follow—through the forest, of course—to another road, a road that would really take them "home." The commander was about to ask Mladen why he kept saying the word "home" as if it were in quotation marks? Was he suggesting the "home" they longed to go back to was only a symbolic "home" that did not, in fact, exist? But before he had the chance to ask, Mladen said the soldiers were asking him to train another soldier who'd escort him, lend a hand in tricky situations, and return alone to the checkpoint with the information. Mladen, in other words, could go off in whatever direction he chose and the soldiers would rebel here and follow him. But, said Mladen, then hesitated and glanced at the other, who coughed and explained that though most of the soldiers were for a rebellion, there were still a few willing to follow the commander, and he, said the soldier, was one, though the other soldiers had no idea. While Mladen was training him in the martial arts and showing him how to survive in the wild, it turned out the two of them were of a like mind and would never support such treason. "Oh, thank you, thank you," stuttered the commander, hoping he wouldn't go overboard and sob. "So what do you propose?" He mustered the courage to ask. "We'll leave on this 'expedition,'" said Mladen, using the quotation marks again, "but then we'll tell the soldiers what they don't want to hear, that we found no way through and we must stay where we are." "But to you we'll report," said the other soldier, "on the real state of affairs." "After that," snickered Mladen, "we'll put this to rights." The commander knew what Mladen meant: instead of the pile of dead in the wake of a rebellion, he was suggesting we produce the same number of dead by gunning them down.

"We'll discuss that later," said the commander. "And now all you need to tell me is when you'll be leaving." "Tonight," said the other soldier, and Mladen nodded. Only then did the commander remember where he knew the other soldier from: soon after they'd arrived, the second or third day, the soldier had come down with something after lunch, and since a sick bay hadn't yet been set up, the commander allowed him to lie down that afternoon in his, the commander's, room. Soon the soldier was moved into the hastily furnished sick bay, but when the commander went to lie down that evening, the fragrance of the soldier's aftershave was so pervasive that the commander couldn't fall asleep till nearly first light. In the morning he changed the pillowcase, but even then the smell of the aftershave slowly penetrated his nostrils and tugged him from sleep. "Fine," said the commander to the pillowcase, "have it your way, I'll manage on no sleep." He'd have told the pillowcase another thing or two but feared its wrath, yet another furious attack, the chilling fear that it might encase his head while he slept. The commander stroked the pillowcase, it sighed tenderly and curled up under his chair. The

commander was staring all the while out the window;
he knew people might think all sorts of things if they
caught him chatting with his pillowcase, and, worst
of all, if they saw how it listened! His favorite poet,
Margareta Greenwald, wrote "Crazy, here they're all
crazy" in a poem as if she'd read the commander's
mind. Her next line, meanwhile, was: "And I, I am
craziest of all." After this the poem becomes a cheer-
less recounting of her dismay over recently delivered
furniture that could be of interest to no one, though
the poem ended well. Oh muse, it said in closing,
instead of giving words, give of yourself, and fear not,
heaven will not forget you. Thoughts of poetry amid
a raging war can serve as a haven for those who long
for a respite, but not for those who rise up in defense
of their homeland, can they? Ah, here he had to stop,
for none of us could be certain that we were, indeed,
still in our homeland. Since we've joined a continental
union, the question of defense of the fatherland is,
at the very least, questionable; any person from around
here could be dispatched to anywhere within the
continental union, always hoping to find ways to hear
about the only place within the union that feels right.

Perhaps this sounds artificial and complicated, but it is what it is. In this effort to unite everyone, many see a nostalgic call to revive the old European empires. Europe can only be great as an allied empire, they say, and the commander goes along with this cheerfully. Outside awaits a different reality, but he now, somehow, feels better. So when a soldier comes up, grenade in hand, at first he smiles and only later reacts to the shouts of warning, wrestles the grenade away, and, in the same motion, heaves it far into a field. After this he's instantly drenched in sweat and he doesn't immediately register the muffled pistol shot with which, right behind him, the soldier-bomber takes his own life. How could this happen, wondered the commander, how could someone who was an ordinary, regular soldier, summoned to pay his debt to his country, turn into a machine primed to destroy others because he cannot muster the strength to destroy himself? Amid applause from the soldiers he leaned over and brought his ear to the soldier's blood-smeared lips. "Sorry," moaned the soldier, barely audible, "sorry." The commander smoothed the soldier's hair, felt his eyes fill with tears, and knew this was the very last moment he could straighten up, display a disapproving scowl as criticism of a suicidal practice that turns the helplessness of an individual or organization into a massacre of innocent civilians, among whom, this being the greatest paradox of all, there were sure to be those who believed in the same things as did the crazed suicide bomber. The commander straightened up and the applause grew to frenzied chants; the commander began to cry, but fine, now they all perceived his sobs as tears of joy, which, thought the commander, was preposterous. Sobs are sobs, there is no great variation here, especially if his was a case of depression. The commander believed that over the last few years he'd been suffering from serious depression, and the fact that many of the symptoms were identical to symptoms for Parkinson's made him all the more depressed. But now was not the time for tales of medical woes, a war was on and health was hardly their primary concern, though it's silly to ignore the fact that such a time did have merit as far as reducing the physical mass of population, which over the last decades had been trending toward continual growth. The lofty language of politics and statistics was bone-chilling, the soldiers were right to rebel. Command language should be simple, accessible, so that everyone can understand it equally, yet always still a little mysterious. A language with no mystery is not much of a language. Language conquers by speaking to our longing to be conquered, which the language they heard over our radio station had no hand in, or better said, mouth in, for one's language relies on the mouth, and some nose, a little throat. And belly, too, one must admit, especially in the case of Japanese, though that may simply be how it sounds for those of us who speak no Japanese. Watch any film by Akira Kurosawa, and you'll see all the actors pulling their words up from somewhere deep inside, especially if they need to voice dark thoughts; they sound as if they already know they'll have no energy for much else afterwards. Most often they don't, like Beckett's creations, instead they merely dream of a place where they'll be tranquil and nibble at parsnips while perching on a barrel or a rubbish bin or a little mound where grows (or, perhaps, dies) a scraggly tree. The commander glanced at his watch and thought Mladen and his escort must be so far away by now that the forest around them was arranging its shadows. He wondered whether they'd be able to find anything or whether this war would be remembered as a comedy of errors, for how could their position be described differently: they knew nothing of their location, they hadn't been assigned a main task, and it all seemed to be designed to pick them off, one by one: none of their communications systems worked, the food supplies were dwindling, and then autumn would come, sooner or later, and winter. But he didn't dare consider that horror, there were plenty of other horrors demanding his attention as insistently as household pets. The commander, one might readily say, was a war veteran. He'd fought with several armies under several flags, and had even been in the United Nations Blue Helmets. He could no longer remember whether that was in Lebanon or Gaza, or was it Cyprus? But it had been interesting, he'd earned a lot and stowed his earnings in a savings account, purchased beautiful Persian carpets, tried hashish, and picked up one disease after another in whorehouses where they, apparently, were not overly concerned about regulation hygiene. The commander even now was fond of recalling those big doe-shaped eyes of the thirteen-year-old girls who gazed at him, and sometimes—only once, said the commander—boys who were younger still, but his reverie was interrupted by soldiers howling at his door. "What's this?" roared the commander when he pulled open the door. "What's the racket? Fuck every one of your mothers! Doesn't this say as clear as the nose on your face that I'm sleeping, or have you all forgotten how to read?" He pointed to a piece of paper taped to his door, which said: "Sleeping! Do not disturb!" But the soldiers were far too excited so they ignored him, grabbed him by the arm, and dragged him out. And there, by the checkpoint, the commander was finally able to understand what they were shouting. "People," they barked, "people are coming!" And sure enough, coming up the slope toward the checkpoint were people in a single-file column, long and straggling, so its end, its tail, was still deep in the woods. The commander clutched his head and wracked his brain to recall where he'd left the instructions for the handling of refugees and procedures for asylum petitions. The only thing he could remember was that somewhere toward the beginning it said the host country was obliged to secure unhindered communication for asylum-seekers, which meant, in other words, that they'd need to find an interpreter. But, for which language? worried the commander, and then quickly splashed his face with lotion, combed his hair, donned his black-rimmed glasses, and then settled his cap in such a way that the visor partially shaded his eyes. This was because, like many other men, the commander fancied himself the master of a fatal gaze others could not resist, especially if the gaze came after a long pause, with the slow removal of his glasses. The people in line, meanwhile, trudged up the steep road, and we could soon see that though men were walking out in front, most of those following them were women, children, and the elderly. Nevertheless, the soldiers took up positions around the barrier and trained their weapons on the crowd. You never know when some crazy suicide bomber might burst out with explosives strapped on and pockets full of hand grenades, and it might be a man or a woman, or even a child, or an elderly woman, the appearance of sheer innocence. If this happens the soldier mustn't hesitate, best to shoot first and later ask questions about the supposedly different intentions of the person you suspect. For instance, it's summer yet someone's walking toward you wearing a buttoned-up raincoat or there are bulges on his clothes as he walks toward a car where political leaders are seated—in such situations there's no waiting, shoot first, ask questions later. If this turns out to be a mistake, the security forces will never be wrong. It'll be the suspect at fault, who refused to respect regulations. So our snipers scaled nearby trees while the soldiers who were out in front of the checkpoint put on protective gear and helmets. This is when the men leading the procession stepped forward and walked over to the checkpoint, while the rest waited at a distance of some twenty paces. Silence ruled, only disturbed by the thud of the footsteps of those leading the column, and then they stopped, and, as someone remarked, there were no sounds for a few moments but the buzzing of bees. There's a whole other story to be told about the bees, or wasps, actually; the buzzing had come from wasps. We'd seen bees on field flowers and clover, but they'd do whatever it was they had to do on the flower and then fly back to their hives where the boss was waiting. Beekeepers are watchful, perhaps overly so, but that's how parents behave, and we all remember those moments of anxiety, when, unable to quell misgivings, parents pace back and forth in front of the house, torn between the urge to punish their child and to fling themselves on the kid and lavish it with love. The wasps, of course, have no boss and no one's glad to see them. They are, however, fair-minded and if you don't touch them they'll leave you alone. But woe to him who pokes their nest, and there were wasps' nests all around us, in the trees, eaves, latrine, even under the seats of our chairs. And there were moments during a meal outside the dining hall when you couldn't bring a spoon to your mouth without a wasp clinging to it, even clusters of them. So in the silence— the only sound the buzzing of the wasps—those at the head of the procession, the three men and three women, slowly approached the barrier at the checkpoint. In fact, one of the women was wearing trousers so, as the other two women were in dresses so long they nearly brushed the ground, many at first thought that it was *four* men and *two* women leading the column. Everything became clearer as they neared, and when the see-through blouse worn by the woman in trousers plainly displayed her womanly charms, perhaps a mite too clearly, the muffled cries of the soldiers and their moans on all sides were easy to hear. When the three men and three women came to within ten paces of the barrier, the commander ordered to them to halt—"Stop, stop, STOP!" he barked—and they did. The commander gestured, four soldiers approached those at the head of the column, and while two soldiers stood, guns cocked, the other two checked to be sure none of the arrivals were concealing weapons. They found nothing, but the commander did have to order them to stop searching the third woman, the one in the trousers, because *those*, remarked the commander, are not grenades. Reluctantly the soldiers obeyed and went back to their positions while the commander beckoned to the people at the head of the procession and called them over. The oldest pulled a bundle of papers from his briefcase and handed them, with a grandiose flourish, to the commander. "What's this?" asked the commander, but the man said nothing. He turned and went back to the others. Later we saw it was a list of all the people in the column, both those alive and present and those who'd come to a tragic end along the way, struck down by illness or exhaustion, or murdered. And while the commander was staring at the paper bundle, the young woman in the trousers spoke up. She was, she said, a translator, though this was not her official function; she did it to help these despondent people who'd come out of nowhere and had only one little wish: to seek shelter from the horrors of war and start a new life in peace. "Not so little a wish," replied the commander, but the young woman in trousers missed the irony, so she said, again, that the people we were seeing wanted to pass through peaceably and start life in the country that lay behind the commander's back. The commander twisted to look over his shoulder. Who knows what he expected to see, but whatever it was he didn't see it; instead he shook his head and told the woman he first had to go through the lists. He might have said more but the woman turned and went back to her group. Within moments, the smell of stewing cabbage wafted our way and this brought the conversation to a close.

Among the people from the column, in a number of places by the road, fires were burning under pots where cabbage was, apparently, simmering. When they smelled it, the soldiers stopped being soldiers. They slipped their pistols back into the holsters and tossed their guns up over their backs, and then slowly, robot-like, as if spellbound, they moved toward the kettles. The people from the column burst into cheers, the girls spun around them dancing and yelping, the men passed around brandy, the older women ladled cabbage and meat onto plates, and soon only the commander was left standing by the checkpoint, facing the young woman. "Not a fan of cabbage?" asked the woman, in an oddly familiar tone. The commander's brows shot up in surprise. Indeed he was not fond of cabbage, but how could this young woman know that? He tried taking a closer look at her, but he was afraid he might become mired in her treacherous, quicksand eyes. A half hour, thought the commander, I give the soldiers half an hour to gorge on cabbage and then I expect them back; the ones who stay longer will be punished accordingly. The woman said nothing, her nostrils flared, but the soldiers, as if they'd read their commander's mind, straggled back. After a time the earlier order was restored and the soldiers formed a semicircle, standing between the refugees and the checkpoint. The leaders of the column had also returned, so next to the commander, near the barrier, only the woman was left who, as she'd said, was a translator, though she hadn't said a word yet in the other language, whatever language it was. In fact, when he stopped to think, he realized none of them had heard a single word in the other language, and when the soldiers were asked whether they'd recognized the language of the people with whom they'd drunk brandy and eaten cabbage, they said they'd heard only exclamations such as "Aha!" and "Oh ho!" and an array of sighs, but they'd communicated mainly through gestures and mimicry. One soldier said that an old woman, when she saw how much cabbage he'd eaten, exclaimed "Ooh, la la!" but it would be difficult to deduce that she was French. They all agreed the cabbage was tasty, the meat delicious, the brandy smooth and clear, which some soldiers held to be a virtue while others felt it a serious flaw. There's no way to please everybody all the time, said the commander when they informed him. He hadn't had the chance to taste the cabbage himself but he did discuss with the lady translator all the details about going through the lists and confirming the identities of the men, women, and children in the column. At first when the woman heard what documents would be required to qualify for refugee status, she was dumbstruck, and it was only through a huge effort of will that she suppressed sobs in front of the merciless commander who, it should be said, had never been merciless, but, when necessary, could put on a convincing act. He was every bit as disturbed, it should be said, by this as she, if not more, and he hastened to draw her attention to the subsequently appended guidelines, including one that stated that in cases where there were difficulties in obtaining the documents, it would be possible to proceed with the go-ahead of the authorized military officer as long as the refugees were willing to sign statements by which they agreed—should they fail to produce the necessary papers within a reasonable time period (not precisely defined)—to return to their country at once. The lady translator rose and went over to the people in the column. She addressed them, and after her speech many of the girls began dancing, waving to the soldiers, and beckoning to them to join in. But seeing the commander's scowls, the soldiers didn't dare overstep the rules. However, when night fell, everything changed. One by one, the soldiers drifted off down the hill to where the girls and younger widows were waiting. The first couples walked off together seeking denser shadows, the seclusion of trees and bushes, but the later couples, eager, presumably, to waste no time, made love right there on the spot, without even trying to hide their nudity, so a passerby would've had the impression of a sea of sighs, keeping in mind that the "sea" air smelled not of salt but of rank sweat and other secretions. At least that's what the commander smelled when, an hour or so later, he tried to ascertain where his soldiers had gone off to. It was when he stood up, pressured by an overfull bladder to make his way to the little room where the toilet buckets were, that he saw that the soldier's quarters were empty and he was hardly able to persuade the guard to tell him what was going on. Then the commander strode off into the dark. As he went down the slope, leaning slightly back to keep his balance, he thought he might be approaching a bizarre beast that was gobbling and slurping in the dark. He unbuckled his holster and pulled out his pistol. This was not a single beast but an entire herd, thought the commander, because the panting and guzzling were reaching his ears from many sides at once. It would have been easier had he brought a flashlight; as it was, with no light, the only thing he could do was strike a match. And then, in the flickering matchlight, he saw that what he'd been hearing was not the slapping of waves but the slap of thigh on thigh. The matchstick was meanwhile burning down and scorched his fingers. The commander swore under his breath and, in a sweeping arc, swerved to stride back up to the barrier. Here the stories begin to diverge and there are several versions of what happened next, but it would appear that the closest to the truth is the one according to which the commander—infuriated and disgusted—flew into his office, where he also slept, snatched a flare gun, ran out and shot a flare off high into the sky. The flare was white, and when it blazed it cast an unnatural light on the dozens of naked and half-naked couples engrossed in their very natural activities. In some places two or even three couples formed larger, entwined groups, which writhed and tossed as if this were the end of the world. The flash quickly fizzled and the commander felt the kind of nausea that usually comes before vomiting. Then he heard men's shouts and women's screams and several shots. Then there was nothing more till the commander heard voices approaching. The commander spun around to find somewhere to duck into, but all the hiding places were too far off, so he chose to crouch behind the concrete pillar to which the barrier was affixed. This wasn't much of a hiding place because no matter which posture the commander assumed, a part of him protruded from behind. In that sense, thought the commander, I'm willing to sacrifice my backside, but luckily it turned out the sacrifice wouldn't be necessary because the voices he'd heard belonged to his own men. They were coming back from down below, chased away by the young women's relatives as well as others from the column. And they weren't just chased away, the commander realized, but several of the soldiers had been beaten up. And, what's more, as one of the corporals dared to add, one of our men was killed. He uttered these words in a heavy, sad tone in which there was a trace of a sort of relief, probably because he'd passed on the terrible news and was now free of it. I'll give you relief, thought the commander, you scum! "Is this how I trained you?" he growled. "Is this how one of ours is at the mercy of the enemy?" The soldiers said nothing. "In ten minutes," said the commander to the two corporals, "I want everybody out here for inspection." The corporals saluted stiffly and began chasing after the soldiers and shouting. The soldiers were in boxers and undershirts, barefoot or in stockinged feet, and driven by the corporals' cries they dashed into the barracks for their uniforms. All this went on in the blackest of darkness, but ten minutes later when the commander strode out to face the men, no one could have said that only a quarter of an hour before they'd been lying between the women's spread legs. Sound travels farther by night than it does by day, so the commander spoke in a mess of hisses and whispers; he was later, for this, dubbed The Snake, a nickname he was proud of, though no one, including him, knew exactly why. Whatever the case, the commander hissed at them from the dark, threatened them, and called them names, and then he switched to a solemn, slow whisper in which he lectured them on how none of our soldiers, living or dead, must be abandoned to the wiles of the enemy. "Maybe by now they've devoured him," said the commander in a solemn tone, as if he actually knew that the refugees at the foot of the hill were cannibals. In the dark someone could be heard retching. "Soon," said the commander, "the sun will be up. I order you to bring him back here when the day dawns, have I made myself clear? And I don't give a damn how many victims there'll be. Understood?" "Yessir, as you say, sir!" hissed the soldiers in response. Only one voice rang out distinctly, "Whose victims, Commander, sir?" The commander stood on his tiptoes as if to peer better through the dark and answered: "Any more stupid questions?" Someone giggled like a frog, but a hush, after this, reigned. "At ease," ordered the commander. Just then, to the east, right over the pointy conifer tips, the sky began to redden and the shadows, hidden until then by the dark, began shivering with anticipation. In no time they'd be venturing into the world, all they needed was to be told whether to go in front of or behind the soldiers. Shadows have a way of moving slowly and faltering, but when they finally make up their minds, their resolve is legendary. And so, when the soldiers set out on their "punitive expedition," as the commander noted in his ledger, the shadows followed *behind* the soldiers, fused to their heels. When the soldiers returned, the shadows were still swinging from their heels, but with none of the earlier joy. In a word, the shadows on that brief journey downhill and uphill aged quickly, perhaps a little too quickly. Anyone would have aged who'd seen what the shadows saw; it's enough to say they became darker, more somber, more hermetically sealed. Who knows what they might have said if only they'd had skill with words. As it was, wordless, they were as mute as the soldiers were who, when the "punitive expedition" was over, returned to the checkpoint. The soldiers had completed the task as they were ordered to, meaning that when they entered the "refugee camp," first they shot at whoever they thought might be the suspicious element, but the deeper in they went, the more suspicious elements there seemed to be, because—as one of the soldiers put it—"not a single person, no child, no one smiled at us with either lips or eyes; their eyes flashed only scorn, a horrible feeling for us because we were there, after all, to protect them, we were promoting their well-being." Was this why the military weaponry was silent only when they were reloading? Or was it tricky for them to choose between several equally attractive and potentially menacing targets, such as, say, a young woman slipping her hand into her bodice to offer a breast to the baby in her lap when she might, after all, have been reaching for a hand grenade, or a young man opening a cardboard box with toiletries while searching for hand lotion, who might have been about to do the same. At such moments they had to react in a fraction of a second and, regrettably, errors were possible. The commander wrote almost these very words in his letter addressed to the organizational committee of refugees, refusing to speak with the lady translator who was howling hysterically, cursing, threatening and repeating, parrot-like: "To kill so many innocent people for just one murdered soldier! Scandalous!"

To this the commander said: "Well, maybe so, but still our suffering and pain matter every bit as much as yours. You cannot insist that we respect your tears while you don't blink at ours. And besides, we aren't the reason you left your hearth and home, is that much, at least, clear?" Not even the commander had an answer for that, not only because he didn't know where they'd come from, but because his every mode of communicating with headquarters and his senior officers was down. The war might be over, but then again it might be ratcheting up, which could easily lead to new alliances, with yesterday's foes becoming, overnight, today's friends. In other words, maybe we shouldn't have been doing what we were doing, maybe the barrier should have been dismantled and passage opened to everyone; or was it just as likely that the barrier would be overgrown with ivy and other vines and never raised again? A wiseguy would say that the real barriers are the ones within us, and that the external ones, like the checkpoint, are, in fact, futile. *Mumonkan*, an ancient collection of Zen tales, speaks of all this with eloquence, but no one among us soldiers had Buddhist texts in mind, especially none of the amateur soldiers, society's dregs, who were generally blasé about warfare. Professional soldiers, like samurai, are another story, and among them one may find connoisseurs of the *Mumonkan* and *Hagakure*, even lovers of the poetry of T. S. Eliot and the music of Edvard Grieg. Yes, it is one thing to be a samurai and altogether different to be an ordinary recruit who, when he opens his eyes in the morning, cares not a whit for himself or for the world. Meanwhile, the sobs and wails welling up from below, increasingly heart-wrenching as the day went on, forced the commander to ask himself, seriously, what to do about the mob of refugees, because, with their actions and, presumably, primitive mourning customs, they were eroding the morale of his soldiers. But he didn't dare forget that seven, if not more, soldiers had already been plucked forever from their ranks, and this was a serious threat to the combat readiness of the unit and our ability to complete the tasks assigned us. By then our numbers had dwindled from the initial thirty-seven to a scant thirty, so duty shifts would be longer and each soldier would have more tasks and greater burdens, but the only thing

the commander could say was to urge us to visit the
little graveyard from time to time, halfway between
the checkpoint and the latrine, to listen to what their
late fellow fighters, now the young dead, had to say.
And sure enough, when we went to the graveyard it
was as if we were stepping into another world. Nothing
separated the graves from us—we'd been thinking to
put up a fence but there hadn't yet been time; we did
install a gate, and everyone who came to the graveyard,
despite, as we said, the absence of a fence, always
stepped in through the gate. The final gate, as the
soldiers so fittingly called it, but in an informal conversation with the commander they made the point
of saying we might add an exit gate on the other side,
so whoever was leaving the graveyard, whether alive
or a ghost, could use it. The commander welcomed
the idea, but immediately said in a stern voice that
there was no place for ghosts in his unit, nor anywhere
else. And then one morning we found a flower planted
on each grave. Not a footprint to be seen. Incredible,
exclaimed the corporal who was assigned the task of
investigating the case, because somebody whose feet
never touched the ground must have planted the

flowers. So what now? Were we supposed to start believing in angels, and was it even possible to believe in angels if we denied our belief in ghosts? "I will not hear talk," said the commander, "of such things." He didn't care; others could decide according to their own needs and beliefs. At first we tried to establish why each particular flower was chosen: why was a violet planted on the grave of the soldier who'd been hanged, while on the grave of the corporal there was a tulip. On one of the graves there was a cactus, while the flower on another looked a lot like a wallflower, and on the last, a daisy. The cactus, of course, was the oddest choice. If the man who was killed had been, say, a Mexican, well then that could have made sense; was it possible the one who did this—one or more, regardless—had known something about these men the rest of us didn't know? In the army you only begin to exist when you report for duty and are issued your uniform; everything that comes before that is nobody's business. Maybe the soldier truly was part Mexican; just as one of us, without anybody knowing, could be Jewish. And if it were found out, what then? The other soldiers would make the man's life a misery is what.

They'd peck at him slowly, the way a chicken snatches and drops a kernel of corn before gulping it down with gusto. And that is how the Jew—hypothetical, or so we hoped—would be snatched and tossed, the difference being that by the end he'd look so bedraggled that no one would care to sniff at him, let alone gulp him down with gusto. The only one who'd fare worse than the poor Jew would be a person who was gay. There are some among us who will tell you a homosexual is the meanest category of human, a degenerate, an incurable lowlife, there's no second chance for him, something you can always offer a Jew—the chance to convert to another faith—and once the Jew adapts (and Jews do adapt so handily to anything), nothing will stand in his way. Chances are a baptized Jew won't become the Pope, but a bishop or a cardinal? Well, why not. We were happier believing that among us there were no such persons, and if there were, well that's a no-brainer—in time they'd give themselves away. Truth is the mightiest weapon, no matter which side we approach it from. But enough about that, we're at war, and such things are better left unsaid, as tales of homosexuals and Jews have long disturbed us. So let's skip the cactus; after all maybe it was just a prank by some childish soul desperate to impress his parents, never noticing, meanwhile, that both parents died years before. Wh-wh-when did that happen? stutters the person, unable to mask his chagrin that he had no idea his parents were already dead. Luckily he didn't blurt something idiotic like: "Why, I was just talking with my father, he says Mother has been under the weather lately." The commander spreads his hands, says nothing. There are moments when words merely confound. And so, when the delegation of refugees came to the barrier once again, the commander refused, at first, to appear, and then, when the cries of the babies in their mothers' arms became too heartrending, out he strode, decked in his parade uniform, and, while the eagle feathers on his cap bobbed before their eyes, he declared, staring up at the sky, "With God as my witness." Rain began falling that very instant and for days afterwards it drizzled. Lucky thing we had no horses: they would not have fared well on such slippery terrain. But should this sudden downpour be understood as affirmation that God exists and was responding? Or was it a spectacular coincidence, as the commander would write in his diary that evening? Meanwhile a new delegation of refugees stepped forward, calm and stalwart, and offered their supplies of meat, sugar, and flour in exchange for beginning the work on their documents of passage. The lady translator was with him again, and she, too, was quiet as a church mouse. "She purrs like a kitten," said the commander when he took her to his office for, as he put it, a "new round of talks." The round lasted just over twenty minutes; when the door to the office opened, the translator and commander were grinning from ear to ear. The commander asked where the priest was, meaning the soldier who'd been a student of theology, and we all froze. Was the commander planning to wed? But it turned out he'd promised the refugees our priest would hold a requiem for the people who'd been killed during the punitive expedition. The chanting could be heard for a while, and when he returned, the priest refused to divulge any details; horror was written all over his face. All he'd say was that there were more victims than we'd thought, and that God clearly was not on their side. Someone yelled that he wasn't on ours, either. "At least he had a glimpse of ours," answered the priest, "and then he shut his eyes." Whatever the case, when the refugees returned to the checkpoint the next day, there was nothing left of their gaiety; theirs was a procession of hollow people and the wind blew right through them. First they came up, one by one, to the table set up on their side of the barrier. There sat a soldier whose job it was to check their documents and fill out the form for each one. The information they were asked was the most basic, first and last name, date of birth, citizenship, blood group, medical history, and so forth. The soldier sat while the person giving the information stood because actually there was no better option. The other chair was taken by the woman who was their translator and who, bleary from the sleepless hours of the night before, kept dozing off and waking with a jolt when she'd start translating everything she could hear people saying around her. Once the form was filled, the person would be given a yellow slip with a number and they'd hand it to the next soldier, the one who manned the barrier. This soldier first entered the number into a large book in which on the first and last pages was written, in large print, "Checkpoint Crossings Register" and, in smaller lettering, the heading: "Entries" on the first page and "Exits" on the other. Then the soldier lifted the barrier and waved the people through with all the belongings they were carrying. There was another table beyond this where sat another soldier. He was also filling out a form, an affidavit for the registered person that in the new place, the name of which was not made explicit, he or she would behave in keeping with the local laws and regulations. The soldier entered the first and last name of the person arriving, after which the person signed it. Then the soldier stamped it, scribbled the information in a volume with nothing written on it, and smiled courteously at the now-registered person, who went over to a third table where sat the commander. He, too, smiled, though his smile was more like a grimace and sometimes faded altogether. Then the commander, leaning confidentially toward the person, would say a few words or sentences and hand them a brochure in several languages about the rights and obligations of refugees, published by the United Nations or some other international body, we weren't sure which. In any case, the commander's brochure made for attractive reading, because most of them who'd crossed over to the other side, to "our" side (though none of the sides of that hilltop were, technically, ours), sat down on the grass and leafed through it, poring over the commander's brochure with rapt attention. The commander protested that the brochure wasn't his, he was merely distributing it, but the moniker stuck, and this only confirmed that popular expressions slip easily into the linguistic corpus of new words or new meanings of old words and there they stay until the next popular new term elbows them out. The day moved on and with it, or rather following it, on moved the refugees who'd been processed. Fortunately there weren't any clashes except in one case when the soldier filling out the first form bumped into the official translator, and she, probably waking from a happy dream, sent him straight to hell and said she hoped he'd hang from the nearest willow. Lucky thing she didn't mention an oak or a pear tree; mythic sites like these should not be invoked in just any sentence, and even the mention of the willow was a little iffy, what with all that goes on with willows. A few minutes later the lady translator, as soon as she'd splashed her face with cold water, realized how rude she'd been and hastened to find the soldier, meaning to apologize. But by the time she returned to the table, she saw another man there and heard from him that the first ("your soldier," the other soldier called him) had finished his shift and probably, said the soldier, had gone off to catch up on his sleep. The lady translator thanked him and headed for the sleeping quarters. If she'd known what awaited her there she probably wouldn't have gone, but, as she later explained, she thought she'd run into the soldier at the door to the dormitory, rattle off her apology and expression of gratitude, turn around, and go. But the soldier was already there, lying on his cot and masturbating. This is certainly not unusual for soldiers, some of them masturbate several times a day, and group masturbations have been recorded with each soldier jerking off the soldier next to him, sometimes two at a time. It's harmless fun, masturbating, harmless yet handy, since it eases tension, promotes physical relaxation, and stimulates the appetite. The soldier may not have known any of that, or was perhaps still unaware that she was standing there, or he may have been confused; whichever it was, when he came with a sigh and opened his eyes, he saw an attractive woman smiling down at him. His next move might be startling, but it certainly isn't difficult to comprehend. He reached out swiftly with his left and grabbed her by the neck, and then, as he drew her to him and pushed her head down, he lifted the blanket with his right and exposed his half-erect penis. Later, when questioned, he did say it hadn't occurred to him that she might be a genuine flesh-and-blood person—what, after all, would such a beautiful woman been doing in their quarters?—and only when he felt, and we quote, "her velvety lips on the head of my penis," did he let loose. He pulled her head lower still which apparently so flabbergasted the woman that she fainted and sank to the floor next to the cot. The soldier wasted not a moment. He woke up a soldier who was asleep on the cot next to his and to whom he owed money—the sum in question was not stated—and asked him whether he'd like the debt returned in kind. The other laughed and, we quote, "told him to fuck off" and turned over, hoping to go back to sleep, but then the first soldier explained what he was up to and pointed to the insensate woman lying there on her back, her legs spread as much as her short skirt allowed, but enough so that at the top of her pale thighs they could see a flash of white panties and around them, strands of curly pubic hair. They grabbed her by the hands and feet, swung her up onto the first soldier's cot, and then, first one, then the other, they shamelessly violated her. Later they claimed the sex was not against her will, that, in fact, she was awake the whole time and loved every minute of it, and as proof they said that during both, and we quote, "fucks," the woman smiled blissfully and she only started screaming, writhing, punching, and scratching when she realized it was coming to an end. If they'd been able to find a third soldier, said the first two soldiers, the woman, and we quote, "would have gladly gone right on fucking," which the woman denied as the most appalling accusation she'd ever heard. The commander, to whom they turned immediately afterwards, had no idea at first how to respond, as his mustache leered while the soldiers were telling him how they'd raped her. And besides, hadn't he been alone with her for a full twenty minutes or more, and hadn't both of them been grinning when they left the office? Was there a valid question as to whether the commander could be partial as a judge? This is a tricky one. Rape of the civilian population, regardless of age or sex, was punished severely, often by firing squad, but the commander was already undermanned and to give up two more men was a luxury he could not afford. When the translator heard his decision she nearly exploded, but by then the matter was done and dusted, and the commander no longer paid her or any of the remaining refugees any attention. They had all been issued their certificates of refugee status and could move forward. Theoretically speaking, they could have moved backward just as well, but nobody considered this as an option. In war one leaves at a run; it's only in peacetime that one approaches at a walk, and we are now, as the commander put it, "up to our necks in war shit." One of the two remaining corporals is supposed to have said: "Shit is shit, there's no divvying it into war shit and peace shit, because then army asses would be different from civilian ones." Wise words, no doubt, and they even coaxed a smile from the commander when someone reported them to him, though later when asked, he'd forgotten them. Forgetting is a marvelous defense, one widely known for years, but not everybody knows how to utilize it well. First of all the mind should be in passive, not active mode, in a mode known as standby, like a printer awaiting the print command. Power usage is at a minimum while the device is forever poised for action, something that is especially key if considered from a military vantage point. And does any other vantage point exist for us? From the checkpoint we watched as the refugee column snaked farther and farther away and then pivoted and disappeared into the forest, but unlike the scout squads that had followed the same path and had circled back to us, the refugees never again appeared, a fact that vindicated those who'd been claiming from the start that the forest was enchanted. Those who did not believe in miracles, and there were plenty of them though the number was dwindling, claimed there were many forked paths in the woods, and whoever knew their destination and knew the woods well, as did the refugees and their leaders, would never stray. Their feet would take them, so to speak, wherever they needed to go. Here Mladen chimed in to say that every forest has a thousand faces and the faces can be easily confused, but the claim that he'd lost his way or taken a wrong turn was highly unlikely. He, at least, knew this, he said, since he was born and had spent most of his life in a forest, on a mountainside, so as far as he was concerned, as with Tarzan long ago, the true wilderness was the city, a claustrophobic urban space. The forest was a different story, and he could go on and on about it, but this time he merely wanted to make the point that there are paths and byways in forests that meander, meaning they take some travelers in one direction and other travelers in the opposite or a different direction. While he was saying this, the other soldiers exchanged glances, shrugged, and tapped their temples. Many might say he was crazy, went on Mladen, but he dared each of us to go off into the forest following the same path the refugees had taken and we'd see whether we caught up with them or whether this seemingly meek path would take us to the shore of a lake, and then slam shut behind us and condemn us to a lifetime by the lake, living off fish and blueberries. Those who spoke up before him suddenly rebelled and said he should stop the gibberish; Mladen dismissed them with a wave, he spat and swore, and this caused a groundswell of protests and threats. Who knows what would have happened in the end if they hadn't heard the roar of a motor and before their eyes appeared a clanking, old military jeep. The jeep clattered up the hill with effort and reached the checkpoint where it stopped, and from it stepped a portly soldier holding a large cloth sack. He strode over to the commander as if he knew him well, handed him the sack, smiled, and, clear as a bell, said—all of us heard it—"Your mail, sir." Though we'd all heard it, each of us repeated the words and soon our unit was humming like a beehive. It's difficult to say what kept us from charging the portly soldier and our commander, ripping the sack from his hands, tearing it open, and dumping the letters on the ground. No, we all stood there quietly and pretended the sack interested us not at all, that we weren't soldiers but, say, beekeepers at an inter-city competition lasting only a day or two where nobody expects to receive mail. So we waited for the portly soldier to exchange sentences with the commander, at least two of which we couldn't catch, in three we grasped a word or two, while the others were fully comprehensible. Short exclamations (and one quite innocuous swear) didn't count, such as: "You don't say!" "Heavens to Betsy!" and "Screw your granny!" The portly soldier sat in the jeep, beeped his horn in farewell, turned the jeep to go back where he'd come from, honked again, revved the motor, and swiftly vanished. For a time the softer and softer hum of the motor could be heard from the forest, and finally that, too, was gone. The commander breathed deeply, took hold of the sack and opened it gingerly as if thinking he might want to use it again. The soldiers in formation were shivering like drug addicts in crisis; their knives, with which they were poised to slice their packages open, kept dropping from their hands. Hearing the clatter of the knives, the commander offered his apologies and even mentioned the tendrils of arthritis that toyed with his fingers and prevented him from being more spry. While he was saying this he drew out the first letter and read the name of the addressee. No one responded and only after the third call did we realize it was for the sentry who'd been found dead in the latrine. "Idiots," said the commander. "Again they're shirking their duties!" He was thinking, of course, of the service that was tasked with informing the families of soldiers who'd been killed, and which clearly was not doing its job. If they had, no one would have been writing to the dead boy; the army did not deliver mail to heaven. Or hell, whichever. For those sorts of messages one needs angels or devils, depending on which variety seems preferable. The commander went on retrieving letters and calling the names, the soldiers came up and took them, some with hands trembling, some with lips contorted, two or three sniffling, and one soldier dropping a proper tear on the commander's hand, the hand that was giving him the letter. For a moment the tear lingered there, then it began to slide, and finally it rolled off and dropped to the ground. The commander had tried to catch it midair but failed. "No point in wasting tears," he whispered, which might have sounded to somebody like a transmission of secret messages and ancient lore. Then the commander took out two letters and crowed: "This is for me! And this, too!" It was obvious he'd be happiest racing off and settling into a cozy corner and there, in peace and quiet, read both letters. But the army is the army, duty is duty, so all he could do was fold them and tuck them into his pocket. On he went reading out the names and, after the letters, he gave out the larger and smaller parcels, as well as a postal form on which was a message that a parcel that was to be delivered to such and such a soldier had been discarded as it contained forbidden substances. In parentheses there was a handwritten note: "roast lamb, brandy, onions." We all turned to look at the soldier, each of us with a mournful expression. We'd never recover from the loss, this was clear, but first we needed to discover where the mail sack had come from. No one knew where we were, all lines of communication were down, the equipment wasn't working, morale was at a record low, and yet our mail was delivered. How could that be? We asked the commander to explain this to us, it was his job, after all, to inform us regularly on the state of affairs in the theater of war and elaborate on things that baffled us. The commander, however, was hopping around impatiently and could barely wait to retreat to his room and read his three letters in seclusion—the third was the last he took out when everybody already thought there were none left in the sack. "Why this mail?" wondered the commander and, bemused, scratched his head. He, of course, had no idea why, but still he tried valiantly to cobble together some sort of explanation. What he came up with held water so poorly, with the water seeping and dribbling out on all sides, that even the most reticent among us began speaking of a flood. Though not yet a flood, the situation completely changed that night when a downpour began that went on for hours, days perhaps, and showed no likelihood of letting up. At first, while thunder rumbled and fat drops of rain splattered on the roof, we all said how the drumming of rain is such a pleasant sound, how nature breathes better afterwards, how much easier we sleep, and how the windows should be opened and fresh air let in. The next morning when we opened our eyes, the rain was still tapping rhythmically on the roof, as if Ginger Baker were a distant cousin. We got up, staggered around among the cots, rubbed our eyes, and conspired to crawl back under the covers. The commander refused to allow it and forced us to do pointless tasks such as picking up bits of litter around the checkpoint barrier. The soldiers who did this came back as drenched as mice. Like the rest of us they had no dry uniforms to change into, and when they stripped off their sopping shirts, jackets, and trousers, they sat there among us half-dressed in their olive-drab skivvies. When he saw this, the commander had an attack of spleen: "What now? Is this a public bath? A soldier in his briefs is not a soldier!" He howled at the top of his lungs, flailed his arms, and portrayed himself, all in all, in an extremely unfavorable light. "But what else could I do?" asked the commander. "Young soldiers are like pups," he went on, "so you must constantly impress upon them who's in charge. Well, will you look at that: our commander is true blue!" He liked this wording and over and over he said: "A true blue commander." In the evening while we were all at work scraping the mud off our boots, he gazed up at the ceiling and whispered: "A true blue commander," and his face went almost translucent with the soft shine of an inner goodness. But according to the quix-otic laws governing the world, good works have less currency than bad, and so it was that the commander's words were drowned out by a sudden hammering on the roof: hail the size of marbles. The thought of marbles stirred a torrent of memories; the wave of nostalgia threatened to paralyze any activity by the soldiers. Had the weather been more agreeable they'd have all been lying on their backs in the meadow and waxing melancholic about the clouds, the shapes and way they were dispersing, how long they last and whether they can be trusted, both for forecasting meteorological events and future events in the lives of human beings. In other words, will the appearance of a pear-shaped cloud affect our life differently from that of a bird-shaped one? And so forth, as one of the soldiers said, with the obligatory stalk of straw in the teeth. The commander, seeing and hearing all this, was devastated. Had he known, he said, what the soldiers in his unit would be like, he'd never have responded to the summons from headquarters. He'd have stayed happily at home and relaxed, calm and serene, in his tracksuit and slippers. Then he wouldn't be listening to this folderol about clouds, or straws. Had someone predicted he'd be commanding a pack of nostalgia-ridden soldiers, he'd have sued this person for defamation, and if he'd done that, where'd he be now? By rights he'd be apologizing to the person and returning the money the person had been mandated to pay him after being so instructed by the court, to compensate for his mental anguish, compounded with interest. "The world sucks," said the commander and kicked a small rock. The rock bounced, knocked the door frame, and rolled out into the damp grass. The rain was still pelting outside, even harder, perhaps, than before, and everything was sinking slowly into mud. Then a soldier whose stomach troubles forced him to venture to the latrine despite the dreadful weather, informed the commander that the latrine was no longer standing; the water and mud had swamped it and swept it down the slope, and the graveyard, too, was beginning to slide, which was easy to see with the lean of the wooden crosses and tilting mounds. Then from deep inside the sleeping quarters rang out a shot and everyone dropped to the floor. "Someone's killed themselves," said a soldier, and—though the bullet had carried away almost half his face—we easily recognized that someone as Dragan

Chicken Little, the youngest of our number. He hadn't had the nickname Chicken Little before he joined the army and arrived at the checkpoint. It was maybe our second night there (or third?), when he'd crowed like a rooster in his sleep so loudly that he woke half the company. The next morning, of course, he remembered none of this, but he stubbornly protested that he'd never dreamt of hens: "Chicks, oh yes," he insisted, "but hens—never!" So that's how he became Dragan Chicken Little and often, when somebody addressed him, he'd answer with a cockcrow, which, without fail, sent us into gales of laughter. Now his body lay there at the end of the room and blood and chunks of his brain and skull were sprayed across several cots. And the near wall. When they saw this, many soldiers ran outside and vomited for a long time into the mud. The commander was the first to collect his wits; he made his way over to where Chicken Little's body lay, then stopped, in disbelief, knelt beside him, leaned over, and whispered: "Why, Chicken Little, why?" Blood trickled onto the commander's right knee and when he rose to his feet we could all see the dark-red stain on his pants. "How are we going to bury him in this weather, with all this mud?" wondered one of the soldiers, and only then did we notice the rain had stopped. The rain stopped, but then something else could be heard, a shrill cry, either animal or human. As always in such situations, there were differences of opinion: some believed it was human but they couldn't agree on what steps to take. Some called for a rescue team to be sent out while others urged caution and even spoke of a trap. The ones who believed an animal was making the sound showed no great compulsion to go outside, yet there were some among them who said there's no serious difference between animal and human suffering, and if they'd go outside for a person, they should do it for an animal. Just as a brawl was starting to erupt with shouts of "C'mon! C'mon!" someone out-shouted the ruckus with the question: "And what if the dead are rising from their graves?" In the sudden hush that followed, no one dared even lift their head to look others in the eye. The shrill cry continued, but now there were brief still spells, respites perhaps, as the wounded animal or mutilated woman gasped for breath and stared into the dark, and every rustle signaled the nearing end, the touch of a cold knife or a bullet's hot steel. That was certainly better than lying there not alive or dead, in the dark, on the wet grass and oozing mud. And who knows what would have happened next had the petrifying cry not fallen silent, followed only by the rustling of leaves in the dark, which always lulls one to sleep, perhaps not as readily as the touch of a beloved hand, but very well indeed, never better, and this may be what the commander was thinking as the soldiers, fully clothed, slumped onto cots and drifted off to sleep. In the end the commander was standing there alone, surrounded by a company of sleepers, and only then did he remember that there was no one manning the sentry post. He tried to jostle one of the corporals awake but the man turned over onto his other side and went right on sleeping. Another corporal, asleep on the next cot over, didn't move at all. The commander rose to his feet, pulled on his boots, grabbed the first gun he could lay his hands on, and sat down outside by the barrier. Aside from the moon in the sky, nothing was moving as far as he could see. Something rustled at his back, then to his left, then to his right. Had he been in Australia, the commander might have imagined a kangaroo seeking its way in the dark, but here at the checkpoint barrier this could only be a grasshopper. Or a jumping mouse, thought the commander, if there are jumping mice around here. All manner of things are in these parts, but there's no one at hand to inform us about them; the number of people who have the gift of the gab, let alone storytelling, has shrunk to next to nothing, and this is not only because of the war. The commander, who'd never been compelled by linguistic subjects and dilemmas, dozed off, but then he felt a touch on his back and, lightning fast, clutching his gun, he turned and peered behind him. No one. The last wisps of scattering clouds were drifting off, and, in no time, under the light of the vast moon, the night was nearly as bright as at daybreak. Soon the commander could see the soldier was right: the latrine sheds lay in pieces on the ground. The graves, however, were not in such bad shape, though some of the signs and one of the crosses were indeed listing. The commander saw all this from a safe distance, from the paved road, because on all other surfaces the mud prevented any sort of movement. Then to the east, the sky began to redden and erase the gray nuances of the remaining, thinned darkness. The commander waited a moment longer, just enough for the top of the sun's orb to appear out of the nest of dawn, and off he strode to the sleeping quarters, banged the iron bars on the soldiers' cots and woke them up with barking shouts. The soldiers, rolled in blankets like huge worms, opened their eyes reluctantly, some even swore while others flung bits of papers with comments written on them, but soon the commander's voice soothed them, and in the end the only noise was the gasps of those who still hadn't finished getting dressed and fumbled at buttoning up their tight trousers or tugging at the elastic band around their neck as they adjusted their tie. The commander ordered them to line up in the narrow passage between the cots, because once they stepped outside the mud wouldn't allow them back in. Then he clambered up onto a cot, coughed, and said: "Soldiers, I'll be brief. The moment nears when our stay here will be threatened by a lack of food, and we aren't much better off with water supplies. All our means of communication have been dead for some time now. We don't know whether the war is still on, or whether one war might have ended and another begun, just as we don't know the main thing—who our enemy is—and this places us in a remarkably awkward situation. Because of all this, I've decided that as of tomorrow, or perhaps the day after, depending on how long it takes for the mud to dry and form a crust, we pack our things and make our way slowly back. Is that clear?" barked the commander, and from all the soldiers' throats rang, "Yessir!" "And now," said the commander in a gentler tone, "let's each of us see to our tasks." He climbed clumsily down from the cot and probably would have fallen if the soldiers hadn't propped him up. He jerked away from them, however, almost angrily, as if his graceless leap was all their doing; he was the first to venture out. The soldiers surged after him though none of them were sure what their tasks were, and they weren't asking anyone to figure out what they should be doing, but they had nothing to worry about: we are usually assigned tasks by others anyway. While the soldiers were streaming out, crowding around the barrier and stretching in the warm rays of the sun, one of them glanced over at the forest, not the trees nearest to them but the woods on the other side, near where they'd found the tattered scrap of fatigues, and having spotted a flash of something, he saw a sniper in the bushes who was taking aim at them. "Sniper!" shouted the soldier and threw himself to the ground, while at that same moment the soldier standing next to him suddenly sputtered as blood spewed from his gullet in a great gush. Chaos. The soldiers dashed back in and out they flew with weapons, dropping to the ground, into the mud, and firing off their guns in all directions. The commander ran around among them in great agitation, and railed: "Where is he, that little mummy-fucker, where's he hiding?" The sniper wasted not a minute, and, instead, calmly, as if at a firing range, he picked off moving targets. Two more soldiers fell before somebody—no one would ever find out who— hit him. The sniper was, apparently, wired to an explosive device because his stagger and fall set off a thunderous, multiple blast. The earth, leaves, branches, and, probably, bits of the sniper flew through the air. The surrounding underbrush burned where he'd been hiding—well, actually, smoldered. The soldiers rejoiced, they jumped, yelled, and pranced around in a circle like Indians around war drums, but then they heard a rumbling, so they stopped and, bewildered, peered into the facing forest. "Impossible," said the commander, but the corporal who was standing next to him said: "Oh, of course it's possible." Afterwards, once a tank had come crashing through the bushes, no one said another word. In silence they watched the gun barrel shifting on the tank with a slight wobble until it fixed on them. And, as if under a spell, they stood and gawked, and one could almost hear the soundtrack from that science fiction series and the phrase: "Resistance is futile." "Not so," whispered the commander, who dropped his weapons, grabbed a helmet, and off he raced into the woods. Meanwhile, without moving its gun barrel, the tank rolled slowly toward the checkpoint. This was one of those light tanks, maybe a British Scorpion, but to the paralyzed soldiers it seemed like the largest armored vehicle they'd ever seen. Then two things happened: first the soldiers caught sight of the commander decked out in green camouflage with twigs on his helmet, slithering through the tall grass, bushes, and mud, making straight for the tank. The soldiers began shouting words of encouragement, which, of course, was all wrong, because the tank crew peered out through various apertures and, apparently, saw the commander; they tried shifting direction but floundered even deeper into the mud. The front part of the tank sank almost to its full height, the gun barrel dangerously close to the ground, and no matter how the caterpillar treads whirred, the tank couldn't right itself. Nothing could stop the soldiers now, and with boisterous cries they charged the tank. Hearing their shouts, the commander scrambled up, sprinted over to the tank, and then cautiously approached the hatch. The bullet that struck him did not, however, come from there but from the forest where, earlier, the sniper had hidden. The commander reeled but succeeded in twisting so he fell not to the ground but slid by the cupola and remained leaning on the tank. The soldiers who were about to charge abruptly changed the direction they were running in and dropped to the ground. One of them did run up to the tank, shove the barrel of his automatic weapon into an opening, and fire into it in several directions. He withdrew the gun, huffed into it like a cowboy into his pistol, and waited. Nothing moved, no voice was heard, only the commander's moans reached us like the buzz of a pesky bug. Meanwhile the soldiers who'd flung themselves to the ground squirmed toward the bushes, approaching from all sides and then, simultaneously, like a well-oiled mechanism, strafed them up and down. When they stopped shooting, they crawled slowly, one by one, into the bushes and we held our breath, fearing surprise. Every shrub might be a deadly trap, we learned this in our military training, so we clutched one another's hands, bit our lips, and shut our eyes. It turned out this wasn't necessary because the soldiers soon returned with the bodies of the enemy who'd been killed. From the tank we pulled another four, so there were six enemy bodies laid out on the ground by the barrier. The commander, who'd only been grazed by the bullet, rifled through their pockets, bags, and gas masks, but nowhere did he find any indication of their identity, place of residence, marital status, or blood group. One of the corporals said to him that though this might be sheer coincidence, two of the enemy soldiers, the two in the middle, were the spitting image of a neighbor of his and the man's son: the same chestnut hair, the same scraggly whiskers, the same arched brows. "I cannot believe they could be anybody else," said the soldier, "but if they are, why are they in cahoots with the enemy? Maybe," he continued, "they're actually on our side and thought we were the enemy when they attacked us?" "No," said the commander, scowling with pain. "Our army has no British tanks." "Then," said the soldier, "apparently they joined forces with the enemy." "They didn't join forces," said the commander, "they *are* the enemy. We're in a new war now; the other one ended but we were never informed." "So what do we do?" asked somebody. "Go home?" "No," answered the commander, "we wait." He assigned soldiers to dig the graves for both our casualties and theirs—ours, each with a separate grave, and theirs, in a single pit. As long as it's large enough, said the commander, so their feet or hands don't protrude. While digging, the soldiers grumbled. Soldiers generally grouse about things, especially things they'd rather not be doing, and who likes digging a pit for a mass grave anyway, especially a proper grave, which means it must be deep, meaning they had to excavate a vast quantity of dirt. Yes, the soil was soft (and fragrant) after all the rain, but soldiers' shovels are the size of spades: for each shovelful of dirt that a real digger would excavate with a single toss, the soldiers needed five tosses. This would wear anybody down, not just a soldier, and anyone would muse on their own death while shoveling, and imagine who would dig their grave. This is, no doubt, an anxious task, but keeping in mind what it entails, the soldiers' grumbles are preferable to Liza Minnelli's screams in the movie *Cabaret* while the train thunders overhead. There were no railway lines or trains here, and above them, in the sky, there were no airplanes or helicopters; in fact, there was also no automobile traffic and one really had to wonder what good there was in having a check-point here at all. Sure, a few days ago a column of refugees passed this way, but how often did that happen? Not often, though globally speaking, more frequently than one might suspect. There are places where war never ends or where displacement lasts longer than the average human lifespan. The check-points there are not, as they are here, carbuncles on the face of the planet, but instead they're a basic part of humdrum existence, though, of course, one would find it hard to describe life in a refugee camp as humdrum. Language betrays us when we least expect it to, just as, in a way, the commander betrayed us: keeping an eye on all the frenzied activity around digging the graves, he felt that if this kept up he'd start weeping and wailing. It is nothing unusual to see a soldier crying, as the commander knew, but still he felt he wouldn't be offering the rest of the soldiers a good example if he wept. Soldiers, after all, need a firm, manly hand, and though history does record several interesting examples of women leading armies, not one of them can compare to Alexander the Great, Attila, or Napoleon. We don't know why this is, though we wonder whether it might be an absence of vision, the inability of women to shape a visionary image of the world. Women are masters of detail, and here no man can hold a candle to them (except, perhaps, men whom many don't consider to be men), but they are at a loss if you ask them for a global vision. How much would Attila have accomplished if he'd been keen only on the details in his corner of the world (a different question is how he even knew there was more world out there somewhere). So the commander didn't dare succumb to his emotions: doing so could possibly lead to the ruination of the world. "Our front line remains as was," said the commander, "because no one has told us anything, no one has made contact. If we do something wrong, the misstep will not be ours." By this time the soldiers had dug the graves, piled the dead bodies in, and begun filling them. The commander, however, retreated to his office and by counting on his fingers and tallying, worked out how many soldiers he could rely on. He counted ten dead—nine privates and the corporal—a third of the company. If the enemy returned and attacked them full force, they wouldn't be able to hold out for long. What a pointless loss that would be, especially as they were guarding a checkpoint and they had no idea why they were guarding it or whose it was! They could, of course, retreat, but which way to go? The time had come, realized the commander, to dispatch Mladen again to scout the terrain. And as if he'd known, Mladen was ready to go, dressed in fatigues and equipped with a hefty arsenal of weapons. So hefty that he cut down on food supplies and left the canned goods in his cubby. A well-trained soldier, claimed Mladen, never need worry about food; he will have learned how to survive; the hundreds of plants, insects, and fruits in the forest offered him a varied, vitamin-rich diet. He hadn't mentioned mushrooms, he said, because saying "mushrooms" would make him salivate. And sure enough, a few droplets leaked out of the corners of his mouth. He brushed them away with his sleeve, shrugged, and left. The commander realized he hadn't given Mladen a precise list of things to check, but no matter. With soldiers like Mladen, one could always expect them to go above and beyond. He called a meeting of the command staff, the two corporals, in his office; he was of two minds about whether to summon the stand-in for the corporal of the third squad, but resolved to have a word with him later. He also didn't summon a junior officer who hadn't been showing up and had even made himself scarce during the heat of battle. The junior officer, felt the commander, was ripe for a court martial, or maybe a hospital stay, best not leave anything to chance. He wouldn't be surprised to learn, thought the commander, that the officer had been slipping secrets to the enemy, whoever the enemy was. Wouldn't it be odd if only the junior officer knew who the enemy was? Or maybe he didn't, maybe he merely hoped to give that impression, for the sake of people who appreciate such impressions? The commander looked sternly up and down at the bronzed corporals (they were, after all, outdoors all day long, while the commander sat in his office), and then his expression suddenly changed and the commander asked them if they'd like a shot of brandy. But what are we drinking to, asked one, his voice quavering, as if they needed someone or something to drink to or they wouldn't be able to drink the shot down. "We are here," said the commander, "to set the stage for what we'd need for a hasty retreat if faced with a superior enemy. We're already down by a third, and if the number falls to half or less, we'll be easy pickings for a cull or a massacre." The corporals nodded. "So," said the commander, "any suggestions?" One raised his hand and said he had no suggestions, but he did have questions, and he immediately asked, "Where is the enemy?" As if he'd been expecting this, the commander unfolded a map and laid it out before his corporals, almost as if setting out for them a spread of exotic fruit, kiwis, perhaps, or papayas. The commander lowered his fingertip to the red dot that, apparently, represented the checkpoint. The spot was on one of several small clearings, surrounded on all sides by dark shading that signified forest. The commander tapped the red dot several times and said: "The enemy is in the forest." The corporal was candid in his disappointment. "In the forest?" he said. "Of course they're in the forest, but where?" The commander shook his head. If he'd known, he said, he'd have chased them out long ago; as it was, he had no other option but to hazard a guess like everybody else. This is why he'd sent Mladen off to scout the territory, he said, and everything might soon make more sense. He looked at the corporal and again shook his head. He didn't like the looks of this corporal much, but appearance matters less in war than skill, and the commander had to admit that the corporal was better at leading his squad than were the others. Other, he corrected himself silently, because the third corporal had been dead for some time. Not so long ago, thought the commander, and then realized he was no longer able to gauge how long they'd been there by the checkpoint. Was it weeks? Months? Years? If he'd been alone in the office he probably would have started to cry. Commanders don't cry, he thought, and for an instant—only briefly—he felt a shade headier, though no better. You can't have everything, the commander thought, and told himself that between "something" and "nothing," he'd always choose "something." The corporal meanwhile shifted from foot to foot, swaying like a sunflower, and this made the commander smile; he'd enjoyed nibbling sunflower seeds at the movies. There were always little heaps of the discarded black shells under his seat. He also liked pumpkin seeds, but there was a real skill to nibbling sunflower seeds, and the commander was, in this, unrivaled. Countless times he'd been challenged to duels, but he always bested his opponent in shelling and devouring the seeds. He could hardly wait for the war to end so he could buy seeds from the snot-nosed vender out in front of the movie theater. Meanwhile, the corporal stopped swaying and lowered his head as if listening to catch the commander's thoughts. "Ultimately," said the commander, "I don't see much choice. We die heroically or surrender like cowards and commend ourselves to the enemy's mercy. We could also, of course, kill each other off, Masada-like. No matter which we choose, history will refer to us as heroes who gave their lives for their country." The corporal coughed discreetly and said, "You don't think we might win?" The commander measured him from head to toe: "And you?" he asked. The corporal said nothing. Some questions should never be asked, that's a lesson for everybody, no matter how quickly one person learns and another slowly catches on. He'd have been happiest going home, thought the commander, and then he snarled and chastised himself by the book for such defeatism. He thanked the corporals and when he was about to close the door behind them, the sound rang out of a shell exploding. It shot high above their heads, as if only testing the area that lay below it. A second, the commander knew, would be aimed much lower, with more precision, and the third would strike right among them. And that is what happened; they had nowhere to go. They ran around like headless flies, buzzing and waving with their little legs, but there was nothing to be done. The shells dropped among them like ripe apricots onto the heads of picnickers who'd fallen asleep in an orchard, but unlike the picnickers who'd gather up the bursting apricots and toss them into a barrel for distilling, the shells tossed the bursting soldiers high into the air from where they dropped to the ground and groaned aloud. At first the commander shouted orders, but soon he gave up and swore furiously. He even leaped up onto a table, or rather the bench that stood by the barrier, as if daring the enemy to shell him alone, but then, just as suddenly as they'd begun raining down, the shells stopped. The commander remained frozen atop the bench, half a swear still on his lips. "They've stopped," said someone, pointlessly, as always at such moments. They could suddenly hear the wrenching screams of the wounded and then somebody shouted "Fire!" and everybody spun to stare at the flames licking the roof of the sleeping quarters and blazing up and up. Several soldiers grabbed rainwater buckets and battled the blaze, while the commander focused on the worst task: identifying the dead men. Five soldiers lay in the grass; three of them were dead, two wounded, one of them slightly while the other, as the soldier assigned to the wounded slowly stammered, probably wouldn't live through the night, which was inching in among them like damp into bones. Then they heard shouts from all sides and the commander, who came running over, pistol in hand, saw Mladen emerging from the forest. He shouted to them not to shoot and raised his hands in which he was holding something, and only when he came closer could the commander see what Mladen was carrying: two human heads from whose severed necks the blood still dripped. This, thought the commander as he watched the soldiers press with curiosity around Mladen and his trophies, is the way other soldiers must have pushed and shoved around the first murdered savages. In line with service regulations he should punish Mladen for the unnecessary abuse and torment of enemy soldiers. He didn't know who'd carved that in stone—it was probably somewhere in the Geneva Conventions—but who gave a hoot for Geneva, and how could he deny the therapeutic impact of Mladen's act, because it was clear that the decapitated enemy heads were having a positive effect on the soldiers who had just been through the hell of shelling. One group had already begun tossing about the bearded head (the face on the other head was clean-shaven, though it had a dense mustache), laughing when droplets of blood fell on their faces, and then someone kicked it, and the shrieks of the soldiers became almost unbearable. Mladen turned and saw the commander. He wiped his hands on his trousers, strode over to the commander, saluted, and said: "Private Mladen Sova requests to address the commander," and the commander, to this, replied: "Cut the shit. Sit here and tell me what's new in the forest and would you like a shot of brandy?" Mladen took a seat and asked: "Only one?" "Two if you like," said the commander. "For you, two." Mladen drained the first to the last drop, licked his lips, smacked them, and said that throughout the forest there were, on the move, fighters from three armies, but there were, possibly, even more armies involved. Some were wearing our uniforms, but whether those soldiers truly were ours, he couldn't ascertain. He came up closer to them but they communicated without words, using only mimicry and gestures. He bared his teeth, stuck out his tongue, rolled his eyes, and crossed his hands. "That means," he said, "that they would like to sit down." "If they want to stand," the commander wanted to know, "what do they do then?" Mladen bared his teeth again, stuck out his tongue, rolled his eyes, and spat. "What do you know," said the commander. "How interesting." He, too, spat in the same direction but missed Mladen's spittle. He hit a neighboring blade of grass just as a ladybug was climbing up it. Then he said that any men wearing our uniforms were not our men, because if they were, they'd have been talking among themselves. Our inability to be concise and to keep quiet at moments when silence is a prerequisite for any sort of action is well known. "My impression," said Mladen, "is that all these soldiers, from all three armies, have been left to a free-for-all." The houses they'd seen earlier were burning, and he'd come across murdered civilians and farm animals more often. The commander said this was something he'd never under-stood: to kill a man, even a woman, that he could understand, but a child or a cow? His head couldn't take that in. And speaking of heads, whose were those two the army was having such fun with? Mladen didn't know. He came across the two of them at the end of a path and thought he'd walk peaceably by them, but then they erred and aimed their guns at him and there you have it, a mistake they wouldn't make again. He stood before the commander, smiled, and quaked like a girl who has come to be introduced to her future husband. By then night had fallen and some of the soldiers were asking where they should sleep. The sleeping quarters had burned, the cots were partly charred and partly soggy from the water used to douse the fire, but even if they were all still intact, what would happen if the enemy shelled us again? "Let's take this one step at a time," said the commander, but his head ached suddenly so sharply that he had to shut his eyes. That same instant, as he shut them, he felt himself lose his balance, and he would have fallen if Mladen and the other soldier hadn't caught him in time. They straightened him up and settled him slowly into the nearest chair. It took a vast amount of energy for the commander to open his eyes and then he saw he was among unfamiliar people. They were all in uniform, mainly in boots, and many of them were wearing helmets. In the air he could smell the soot of the doused fire, and the stink of excrement and human sweat. The commander wondered aloud what he was looking for here, but then someone's face loomed, indicated a large hypodermic needle and said it wouldn't hurt. "You've got to be kidding," howled the commander, but too late. He felt the little prick somewhere on himself or near him, he wasn't sure, and when he opened his eyes again it was already morning. And what a morning! Sunny, fresh, drenched in the fragrance of flowers and somehow full of promise. The commander twisted around and realized that he was lying in his cot, in his room, except that above the cot where there used to be a ceiling, he saw a tarpaulin stretched. The chamber pot wasn't where it should have been and the commander thought the soldier who'd failed to bring it in should be punished with at least three extra duty shifts. "The army means order, or it isn't an army," said the commander to himself and then he staggered out, stood by the nearest tree and began emptying his bladder. He squinted with pleasure at the relief this brought him, but suddenly he went rigid and froze. There, only sixty feet from him, was a group of journalists. He was first spotted by a woman in a red dress and red-framed glasses, and then they all turned to him and pointed their cameras and photography equipment, as well as tiny recording devices, in his direction. The commander barely had time to shove his private parts back into his pajama pants and then, as the reporters slowly but surely advanced on him, he thrust out his chest and announced, "Not one step further! You are in a zone that is off limits to civilians, and anything you record, write down, or take pictures of must receive the approval of the military authorities. You'll be given the forms for your request for approval a little later, and there will be a tax to pay for a fee regulated by law." "Just one question," said a tall photographer. "Yes?" said the commander. "Do you accept credit cards?" asked the photographer. "Why, of course," said the commander, and turned toward his room. "If you take a closer look you'll see that Visa and MasterCard are our sponsors." Where did all of them come from, wondered the commander, and who gave them permission to move around the barrier? He thought heads would roll for this, and then he remembered the two heads with which the soldiers had played soccer and he was swept by a terrible crush of shame. Dressed in his uniform, cap in hand, he came out again, but now on the other side of the barrier. Nowhere, however, did he see a single soldier. Not many of them were left, of course, roughly half had already been killed, but still there ought to be at least one sentry on duty. Then he thought: "What if they all deserted?" and suddenly he went pale. Then he had to admit that he wouldn't have held it against them if they had, because they were clearly fighting a hopeless battle. His company was halved, out of the thirty soldiers only some sixteen were still alive. At least that is what his calculation had told him the day before, but that was last night, before he fell asleep, who knows what horrors had played out while he slept. Then someone's words reached him, fragments of a conversation, and when he peered around the corner, he saw all his soldiers. They were sitting in a circle eating cornmeal mush. The junior officer was the first to catch sight of the commander, he leaped to his feet and inhaled noisily, but the commander didn't allow him to speak; he ordered him at ease and said they should go on with their meal. "We're eating cornmeal mush with cheese," said some of the soldiers and the commander decided to join them. Soldiers need, as the commander knew, to see as many examples as possible of officers with the highest ranks and medals doing what they're doing or eating what they're eating. The rank and file was thereby shown that the officers were flesh and blood like them, and despite military hierarchy they were only human. "Real people, first and foremost," the commander liked to say. However, this time he didn't say it because he, too, loved cornmeal mush, especially when mixed with milk, and if there wasn't milk then cheese would do. He turned to look in every direction and only then saw the extent of the damage from the shelling the day before. Had that been only yesterday? It might have been yesterday, thought the commander, or maybe ten days ago. All the days were the same, though the deaths differed. When he dwelt a little more on it, in fact, all deaths are the same, death comes to everyone the same way. As the poet said: "Death will come and will have your eyes." It won't have my eyes, thought the commander, I'd rather pluck them out myself than let death carry them off on its face. A face with nothing anyway, because death is a skeleton that walks and carries a scythe instead of crutches.

Death walks with a limp, and since it's terribly vain, it leans on the scythe as it approaches those who are on its list. It doesn't carry the scythe to cut anyone down because death doesn't kill, it comes to fetch those who are already dead, and the scythe simply serves to channel the flash of light in the eyes of those waiting for it, so that, blinded, they won't have the time to see how lame death is. The commander finished his portion of mush and burped. In another situation he would have asked for seconds, but now there was no time. And besides, he wanted to know why nothing was functioning. Where, for instance, were the sentries? Were the observers in their positions? Had the radio operator attempted to reach somebody? What was the condition of the wounded, and, more important, why had they let him sleep? The commander rose slowly to his feet, cleared his throat, and waited for the soldiers to quiet down. Then again all the questions, adding in the end, as if summing it up, "Who's at fault for this morning's chaos?" The junior officer raised his hand and, without hesitating, said he'd made the decision because it was clear to everyone that this is a pointless battle, a battle that makes sense only if it is understood as an insane clash in which they are condemned in advance to death. "It's obvious," added the junior officer, "that we were sent here with one goal only: to stave off the enemy as long as possible, meaning as long as there were soldiers alive. That's why I decided to free the soldiers of their duties, and we are prepared to surrender to the enemy as expediently as possible." The commander, who until then had been listening closely, his head slightly tilted to the side, howled that this was treason punishable by death and reached for his gun. Before he'd had the chance to unbutton his holster, everywhere around him he heard the chink-chink sounds of weapons being cocked and found he was surrounded by barrels of the most varied assortment of guns, including a mortar. "Fine," said the commander, "I understand." And besides, hadn't he himself thought the very same thing, hadn't he said he wouldn't hold it against any soldiers who deserted? Shooting began just then, and everyone dashed for shelter. They needed a breather to figure out that the bullets weren't intended for them, somebody else had joined the game, renegades or rebels, or the residents of yet another country, in any case someone whom the commander and the remaining soldiers knew nothing about. The commander shouted to the radio and telegraph operator that he should try to locate the frequency of one of the enemies and do what he could to ascertain who they were. A little later, he lay down beside the operator and listened to voices that sounded Chinese, though it could have been any Asian language. The operator turned the dial to other voices, equally agitated, but by then the commander had no doubt. The language was Czech, and the commander thought back with regret to the many trips he'd taken to the former Czechoslovakia, where, for a person who had foreign currency—and the commander had a pocket full of deutsche marks and American dollars—life was cheap, beautiful women were easily accessible, not to speak of the beer. In a word, paradise. Yes, yes, old chap, said the commander to himself, that was the life and not this crap with only death to offer, as if death were something you could taste-test for a few hours and return if it didn't suit you. But there was no answer to the question of whose side the Czechs were on, the same as a question the commander might have asked: whose side are we on? Who is who in this mess, thought the commander, and then a hand grenade, activated, rolled his way. So that's that, thought the commander, this is it, and he decided to let it explode. Then he caught sight of the horrified gaze of a soldier, a boy, lying there next to him, his mouth opening. The commander grabbed the grenade and heaved it as far away as he could into bushes, a thicket, by the path leading to the forest. A little farther off were heard shrieks and cries, and soon a group of soldiers ran out from the thicket, hands held high. The shooting, which had begun abruptly, ended abruptly, and the soldiers trotted slowly up to the checkpoint barrier, which, throughout the melee, was unscathed. The commander rose and went to the barrier. He knew he was standing completely exposed to enemy snipers, he even felt a little itch in the places they were aiming at, his forehead and chest, but as a true soldier, and he felt he was one, he had only one thing in mind: completing the task he'd undertaken and never, remember this, he said to the kids standing by the checkpoint, never show fear. "I am not afraid of death," said the young soldier, "but I am afraid of a gradual, inching death." "And boring," shouted another, "there's nothing so awful as a boring death." The commander felt something tugging at his pant leg and saw that the young soldier had crawled over to him. "I can't get up," whispered the soldier, "because I think I soiled my pants. If I'm wounded and am suffering would you put me out of my misery?" "Stop talking nonsense," said the commander, he crouched and slipped his hand under the soldier's belt, then turned him over on his side and moved his hand to the man's scrotum. When he withdrew it, his hand was covered in blood and excrement. With the same hand he greeted the soldiers who, a few seconds later, hands still high in the air, trotted up to the barrier. He went over to one of them who wore symbols on his sleeve and, waving his bloody, putrid hand in front of the man's nose, asked, "Where from?" "Where from?" repeated the soldier, and shrugged, plugging his nose and breathing through his mouth. "Not ours," said the commander, "that much is clear." "Not ours," echoed the soldier, "that much is clear." The commander turned to his soldiers and asked them what they thought, were these clowns messing with him and what should he do. He received so many suggestions that he could have spent the rest of the day weighing which was best. The soldiers, meanwhile, had chosen a suggestion that someone, sniggering, shouted out: "What about: kill the lot!" and immediately most of the others began a chant, softly at first, of "Kill! Kill!" The commander only then wiped his hand off on the grass and someone's shirt hanging from the barrier post, and then he asked the foreign soldiers whether they had passports. They shrugged and the commander flew into a rage. He turned them, one by one, to face the enemy positions, repeating: "Go there, you'll be better off there." He gestured for them to keep their hands up and gently nudged the soldier who wore the insignia of rank on his sleeve. In the hush that followed, all that could be heard were their agitated voices, and soon, not even those. Whoever was hiding in the bushes on the opposite side let the group approach until they were about sixty feet away, and then a blaze of gunfire erupted as if an entire armored unit were on its way. The commander peered out just when the soldier wearing the insignia was blown toward the checkpoint, probably swept by the force of a strike, and in one endlessly brief moment his gaze found the commander's eyes just long enough for all his bitterness and pain to spill over and for them to communicate the commander's betrayal. "How could I have betrayed you," said the commander aloud, "when you aren't even my soldier?" He shivered because he knew better. Somebody surrenders to you in a plea for clemency, and you, without so much as a twinge, send them to their death. That sentence doesn't read well, thought the commander, no matter which end you read it from. In fact, he thought something different: chaos now reigned and there'd be no turning back. A war is a game in which there are rules to be respected, and as soon as these rules are skipped, the war is no longer a game in which the foes are bent on outwitting one another. Until the First World War, thought the commander, wars were a lot like chess, even the rulers and generals saw them that way. They perched here and there on the surrounding hills and watched how their armies advanced or retreated. Until then a ritual, a theater of manners, a well-rehearsed ballet or operetta, war was now verging on chaos, arbitrary unpredictability, slaughter for slaughter's sake. The commander knew that none of this justified him in the eyes of the soldier, in that immeasurable moment when their gazes locked. But that doesn't mean, thought the commander, that he was flailing or had lost his will. Not at all, indeed he suddenly came alive, rushed from man to man, spurred them with encouragement, offered to be a father or mother to them, and then went over to the young soldier and told him to change his clothes before he stank up the place. Somebody might accuse us of jeopardizing the environment on top of everything else, that we're destabilizing the ecology. He went looking for the radio and telegraph operator but, instead, came across the cook. Everything's all set, said the cook, his stove was working, he had enough fuel, and was about to start flipping pancakes. The commander asked that two with jam be saved for him, and then he spotted the operator. There the man sat on an empty barrel, smoking. "So, do you want to go home," asked the commander, "like those men over there?" The operator looked at him with clouded eyes, and said, "My father died." The commander felt his shoulders and back heave under the weight of his own stupidity and shame. He wanted to say something more to the operator, maybe to himself as well, but all that came to mind was a sentence he'd read somewhere that all words were pointless in such situations, because no matter what a person said, the dead were still dead. A person should not, however, be left without hope, one should continue using one's words. The commander whispered a curse and then asked the radio and telegraph operator how he'd heard of his father's death. "My brother let me know," said the operator. "Your brother?" repeated the commander. "Yes," said the operator, "my brother." "I didn't know you had a brother," said the commander, his voice shaking. "A cousin, actually, my aunt's boy," answered the operator. The junior officer, standing not far from them, said that when a family member dies, a soldier is permitted a four-to-seven-day furlough for the funeral. The operator said he'd go only if he were allowed to travel in his civilian clothes, because in his uniform he was a sitting duck. The commander took a deep breath and asked who would replace him as radio and telegraph operator, and the junior officer said he was prepared to take over the man's duties. His expression was so doleful as he said this that the commander thought the junior officer was about to ask that the father's death be ascribed to him as well. "There is no such thing as double dying," said the commander firmly and sent off the radio operator to change his clothes. He gazed up at the sky: it was crystal clear, endlessly blue, and only here or there was it shrouded in a pale mist. The blue was somewhat paler there, but no less beautiful. What is wrong with me? thought the commander, somebody might think I'm in love. He really was the kind of person who was always falling in love, and this wasn't just from time to time, but regularly, the way a passionate reader devours novels. His civilian librarian was glad for this and told him the poetry collections shelved in the library were surviving thanks entirely to the commander. "No one," said the librarian, "no one reads poetry anymore!" Someone then piped up to ask whether any new poetry is being written. The librarian was about to respond and provide figures from an article written for the recent annual conference of the Librarians' Association, but he was interrupted by an impatient reader who wanted to hear how many readers were borrowing books of poetry. "Well, the commander and . . . and . . ." stuttered the librarian, "and there was a girl who once borrowed Lorca's poems, but she hasn't yet returned them." The commander cautioned them to retreat to their shelters because at any moment the afternoon session of gunfire would begin. The enemy stopped its shooting at around 11:00 in the morning and this tacit cease-fire would last until 4:30 in the afternoon. Why sweat out there in the heat of the day? asked the enemy commander once when they'd spoken to each other over the radio, we have plenty of time for fighting when the sun isn't beating down quite so fiercely. "A genteel man if I may say so," said the commander to the radio and telegraph operator and that prompted him to wonder where the operator was now that he'd sent him to change his clothes. He should be leaving now, thought the commander, because at least one of the enemies won't be trying to kill him. As for the other— or others, who knows how many were out there—he couldn't say. If the united Europe had broken asunder, and if clashes had begun in a number of the countries with pro-European against anti-European forces, it would be realistic to imagine that there might be dozens of potential and/or genuine adversaries. It wasn't clear to him how the radio and telegraph operator planned to get home, but he understood this feeling of misery, self-pity, and self-accusation, because he, too, had been away from home when his father died and until recently he'd been blaming himself for that. As if his father would have survived had he been by his side, thought the commander. He came across the radio and telegraph operator who, dressed in his civvies, was kneeling by his belongings. The commander thought the man might be praying, but it turned out he was actually asleep. The commander touched his shoulder and, bringing his lips to the man's ears, he said: "It's time!" The operator started, rammed the back of his head into the commander's mouth and both of them swore. "Scram," said the commander, "they're about to start." The radio and telegraph operator scampered off down the hill. He stopped for a moment before turning into the forest, straightened, thrust out his chest, and flew into the woods. A little later three shots rang out and though

the chances were fifty-fifty, the commander was almost
certain the radio operator was still running. You could
see right away, thought the commander, that he was
one of those people bullets didn't want to hit. There
aren't many folks who enjoy that kind of luck, though
they'll pay for it elsewhere, as things tend to go with
good and bad luck. Life is impartial, it plays no
favorites. If a person is offered something that is not
equally accessible to all in equal measure, they'll also
be given something bad, meaning they'll be greater
losers in other realms. So the radio and telegraph
operator, say, was spared the bullets, but he often
tripped and fell, and it may have been a fall that
additionally shielded him from bullets. The radio and
telegraph operator may have stumbled exactly when
the fingers of three snipers were on their triggers, and
his tumble removed him from the enemies' field of
vision. But why shoot at him when he was merely
passing through, peaceably, in civilian dress? That is
what the commander wanted to know, and he'd have
given anything to find out who was hiding in the
forests around the checkpoint. At the moment when
the shells began to fly, a thought popped into his mind

that would come back to haunt him many times during yet another sleepless night. And what, said the thought, what if there never was a war to begin with, if all this was just somebody's huge experiment, an attempt to test the mettle of various categories of soldier in an atypical situation? Perhaps the victims had already been marked in some way in advance and they didn't protest being chosen to leave the scene of life so early. The commander curled up in an even tighter ball in his hole, listening to the malevolent whistle of shells. One exploded not far from him and covered him in a mound of dirt. Then silence, and the sound of someone crying. The person wept and shouted a few times: "Mama, oh, Mama!" After a while the weeping changed to whimpering that sounded as if it would never stop. The commander tried blocking his ears, but the whimpering was merciless and nothing could stop it. A little later the enemy's weapons thundered again, and then, when they subsided, there was no more whimpering. It had been a direct hit, the commander later ascertained, but though a complete identification of the remains was not possible just then, he was certain this was the young soldier who not long before, on this very spot, had been sobbing in shame for having soiled himself out of fear. So it is, thought the commander, that nature makes its selection, leaving the toughest and most tenacious, and then his gaze shifted from soldier to soldier, and he had to admit that the demands of natural selection were truly bizarre. He'd expected to see a dozen of the most vigorous soldiers, the healthiest, most robust, most determined, but instead he saw a motley group with the tall and short, fat and skinny, sour and bright-eyed. "How many of us are left?" he asked the junior officer who checked his pad. "All together," he said, finally, "nineteen." "Maybe we should split into two groups," said the commander, "and steal away from here by night somehow." "But," said the junior officer, "which route do we take? There are enemy forces all around us. If we go to the right, downhill, we'll run into the ones who shot at the radio operator: on the left are the ones who attacked us from the forest and did so treacherously, from behind, while facing us are the first enemy units who mowed down that group of unarmed soldiers in cold blood while hitting us so savagely with all their different weapons. If they'd had an atomic bomb they'd have dropped it on us, they wouldn't have even waited to check which direction the wind was blowing, or where it would blow the radioactive dust." "How about over there," said the commander, and pointed to the most distant part of the forest, and a wide meadow near it. "Ah, yes," said the junior officer, "what's there?" "Nothing and nobody," said the commander, "just what we need." "But how do we go from here to there?" asked the junior officer. "Isn't that area perfect for hunting rabbits?" The commander scratched his sweaty head. "If that's so," he said, "we'll have to think of ourselves as rabbits; it's our only way of getting out." "But what about our dead?" Asked a soldier when the commander and junior officer told them of the still half-baked plan. "We can't leave them to the enemy!" "For God's sake," said the commander, "they're dead, and we aren't about to disinter them." "Oh yes we are," shouted the soldier, raising his spade high in the air and calling out, "Who is for taking them with us?" Most of the little spades waved high above their heads. "But if they see what we're up to," the commander played his last card, "they'll know we're preparing to leave." "No, they won't," barked the necrophiliac soldier, "because we'll pretend we're just tidying up the graveyard, and we'll pretend that they are up at the top of the hill and the graveyard is right at the bottom, and they won't have a clue what we're doing." The commander threw up his arms in a gesture of surrender and sat down on the nearest chair. He could do nothing more than look on while the "deadly rebels" marched down to the graveyard. He was suddenly left alone, which had always suited him, but he'd found this easy to forget these last few weeks. Everything is so easily forgotten during wartime, even that commanding officers were ordered to assign duties to their soldiers, preferably in teams, if only a team of two. What matters, as stated the order that was circulated to all the officers who were kept in combat readiness, is that no one be allowed to distance themselves and as soon as someone is noticed growing distant, they should be steered, at all costs, in the proper direction. At what cost? All costs. Yes, sir! At ease! The commander thought he heard gunshots, but when he opened his eyes, nothing. Devil take it, thought the commander, there must be something,

while twigs were snapping behind his back. He grabbed
his revolver and, with the chair, toppled over onto the
ground. He was about to shoot when he saw Mladen
waving his arms almost frantically and shouting something, and the commander barely managed to reverse
the pressure of his finger on the trigger. "Are you mad?"
he asked Mladen. "You could have been dead by now."
"Lightning never strikes a beech tree," laughed Mladen,
and then, looking around, he asked where the others
were. "At the graveyard," said the commander. "Every
last one?" asked Mladen. "Yes," said the commander.
"How did they manage to kill all of them at once?"
asked Mladen. The commander said he hadn't understood the question and only then did he get the gist.
"They're in the graveyard," he said, "but they aren't all
dead." "What are they doing?" asked Mladen. "Bidding
their fond farewells?" "No," said the commander,
"they're readying the bodies for transport." "For transport?" repeated Mladen, astonished. "What? They had
it with war and wounded each other and now they're
lolling around in hospital beds?" The commander
carefully related some of the more recent events and
the moment of deciding they'd leave. "I could no longer

play the rabbit in the hunting grounds," said the commander, and besides, our forces were halved, and fifteen soldiers gave their precious lives—for what? Could somebody tell me for what?" Sounds reached them of excited voices, among them women's. Soldiers soon appeared leading two young women. They'd found them at the graveyard, said a soldier, though it now looked more like an archeological site from the Middle Ages. What were they doing? the commander wanted to know, and did they say anything about this place? We didn't understand them, Mr. Commander, sir, and we think they're speaking the same language the refugees spoke. The commander needed a moment to recall the refugees, but he couldn't remember their language. Then somebody mentioned the lady translator and this drew the commander's lips into a grin that he hastily suppressed, though not hastily enough, at least not for the soldiers standing by his side. No, not that side—his other side. The commander recalled how she'd whispered incomprehensible words in his ear, and later, in a somewhat throatier voice, she'd said them in his language. The commander's cot was narrow and one of them had

135

always been in danger of tumbling to the floor, but she'd twist up high or lean down low, and kept the balance. He wondered, looking at the two girls standing there in front of him, whether they'd know any of these skills, but their free, cheerful glances told entirely different stories. They were the advance team, sensed the commander, but he couldn't sniff out what would be coming after them—a new day, a new human being, or new words, something unheard of. The girls pursed their lips as if they were about to say something, then looked at each other and giggled. Why hadn't the soldiers raped them down by the graveyard and left them there to guard over the emptied graves and toppled crosses? He felt a surge of strength well in him and wondered whether it might be best to pull out his pistol right there and kill them both without a word or any commentary. He even dropped his hand to the pistol grip, but his pistol told him, "Don't you dare! Understood?" "Understood," whispered the commander, and then looked around: it would be terrible if anyone caught him conversing with his pistol. They'd immediately declare him mad, which would be silly—weren't soldiers expected to become one with their weapon, to treat it like a close cousin? In public life this is called a double standard, thought the commander, or: do what I say, not what I do. No matter which way you look at it, life is worth less than a wooden nickel; there's always someone standing over your head and noting what you're doing, turning life into a list like those long lists one writes when going off on the weekly or biweekly grocery shopping. Of course, all this has nothing to do with the army, nothing whatsoever, and yet the army is so vital for everyone. It would be easy to say that the army is foisted on the state like a cuckoo bird's eggs, that society has embraced the army as a necessary evil, except it revolves around the question of war. War is so unnatural, so different from all else, that no one in their right mind can grasp why war would be a part of human culture. The commander turned—he ought to love war at least a little, being a man in uniform, but he couldn't bring himself to. Never would he admit this to his soldiers. But he also couldn't abandon them to this hell. So like a good fairy he hovered over their preparations for departure. Everything was supposed to look as if nothing out of the ordinary was going on, because who could say how many observers and spying eyes were trained on them. The soldiers took turns at their regular duties, the cook cooked up hot dogs for supper, the commander fiddled with the dials on the radio and bobbed his head to the rhythm of the various languages coming over on it. Meanwhile the other soldiers were loading up their backpacks, pretending to inspect the contents or getting their dirty clothes ready for the laundry. The two girls were still alive, sitting on the ground, tied to a tree, while the commander again thought there was only one solution for them: a bullet to the brain. He was horrified by his thoughts, but still he felt his hand jerk and inch toward his pistol. At one moment his fingers even brushed the grip, and the meeting of skin and metal seared him as if it were an open flame. This is a sign, thought the commander, that I must go no further. He turned to look around him but no one was watching, no one speaking to him, they were all busy with their jobs and seeing to their own troubles. Then they switched places, the ones who'd been packing pretended they were sentries and observers, while the others, dodging behind charred ruins and tent flaps, readied their munitions and cleaned their uniforms and boots as if sprucing up for a parade. The evening settled down around them like a sheet scattered with crumbs doubling as stars, thought the commander, and felt he could fall in love at that very moment. It's a lucky thing women don't serve in our army, he thought, and his mouth went suddenly dry though it had just been full of spittle. The commander imagined a girl curled up on the edge of his cot, and he made her turn to face him and smile. She threw off the cover, sat up straight, and spread her arms. Lie down, shouted the commander, lie down! But too late. The bullet struck her on the back near the heart and she flailed as she fell. The commander whimpered as if about to cry, but he held back the tears. He had nothing against tears, he even felt soldiers ought to cry and tears were a handy way of easing burdens, but he also felt that an officer, meaning, a soldier with rank, must never weep in front of his subordinate officers and ordinary privates. Someone else might deduce, thought the commander, that I am strict and squelch feelings, both those of the soldiers and my own, but nothing could be further from the truth, I'm as soft as cotton, thought the commander, or even softer. He poked his arms and legs with a finger, but nowhere did he feel softness. He squeezed tendons, muscles, bones, and skin, but they were hard, firm, and prepared for every possible further turn of events. If you're not prepared for every eventuality, you're prepared for nothing, no matter how differently he might think, thought the commander. He made the rounds of the soldiers and checked each of them, one by one. It wasn't easy. Tears welled, his stomach clenched, his handshake was limp, and his heart, the old traitor, pounded like a rabbit's. "We'll wait a little longer," whispered the commander into each soldier's ear, "till dark, and then we move." He'd squeeze the soldier's shoulder and bring his lips to their cheek. Each time he did, he'd feel the cheek tense, the skin fear his touch. But maybe it's always like that, thought the commander, when a man kisses a man, in war or peace, in an amorous encounter or a farewell to a warrior whose fate was long sealed, this is as unchanging as Greek myth. The commander would have been glad to imagine himself as Zeus, especially as the Zeus who'd turned into a swan, but then he hastily spun around, certain everyone must be eyeing his crotch. The commander was wrong, as was obvious to all of us but not to him because even if we'd wanted to stare at him there, and we didn't, we wouldn't have had much to see. The dark was as thick as dough, affecting every thought we entertained, every step, not to speak of our mood. But the commander had resolved that we'd play the game, he placed his people in positions, ordered us to set out the manikins that were designed, the next morning, to mislead, though the commander knew the deception wouldn't last long, the motionlessness of the manikins would first stir suspicion, and then this would swell until the enemy commander finally chose three or, maybe, four, or even five soldiers—never underestimate the enemy—and in total silence, like true professionals, they'd traverse the distance between their positions and the checkpoint, but in such a way that not a single blade of grass would shiver, not a branch would sway and not a bird would flutter skyward, stirred from sleep or luring those strange creatures away from her nest and fledglings. Yes, thought the commander, as far as birds are concerned, people are indeed strange creatures, nothing more, and if things stood differently, if birds and people truly were buddies, they'd now be hidden away somewhere, carefree and certain that no one would ever find them. No, thought the commander, no one ever will find us, and then, by mysterious pathways, the thought popped into his head that he should whisper a warning to the soldier walking in front of him that if a flare were to be fired off they should freeze and stand that way until the light faded. He added: "Send it on," and he saw the soldier lean toward the soldier in front of him, and just as the message reached the head of the column, they could all see the slender trail of a flare mounting in the sky and then blazing and spreading its phantasmal, wan light across the slope. The rigid, frozen soldiers looked like enchanted ballet dancers in a grotesque dance. Many of them found the muscles on their legs trembling and the light of the flare seemed like it would never dim. But no flare lasts forever, they are all transient, as are we all, thought the commander, as are we all. The soldiers barely had the time to stretch before a new flare had them freezing again, clinging to the nearest vegetation. "Down!" spat the commander to the shadows in front of him, and the soldiers, as if they could hardly wait, plunged to the ground. The flares lit the sky and the clearing several times and then stopped. The dark was still thin for a little longer, and then it thickened again around them like a curtain. The commander straightened slowly, rose to his feet, and drawing his head into his shoulders, strode to the head of the column. Just then they clearly heard the ringtone on somebody's cell phone and the first notes of the popular song "Marina" jangled like a bomb blast. Where had this phone come from when they'd been without electric power for days? "Hello?" said a voice in the dark, and then they could hear the phone being flipped shut. "Wrong number," said the same voice, defensively. "Turn off that piece of shit," ordered the commander. He was doing his damnedest to sound fierce and stern, but it wasn't working because he was also remembering how once long ago at the seashore he'd held a girl with ashen hair by the hand while that very song drifted their way from a hotel. He could even remember the words: "For days I've loved Marina, but her cold glances hurt me . . . ." Then, for the first time, he wondered what point there was to a war in which

you don't even know who your enemy is, or why you're
fighting, or whether a peace treaty has already been
signed, or who will end up envying whom: the dead—
the living, or the living—the dead. Later on, in the
woods, on the ridge, the commander chided himself
for the defeatist thoughts, but they offered him some
brief comfort. To be honest, war is a holy mess, we all
agree, there's no dispute. Every war is like that, the
just and the unjust wars, the wars of conquest and
defense, war on land and war on the sea, and war in
the air and war underground, all of them are the same.
War is shit, that's that, period. Later, on the ridge,
the commander would feel shame at these words,
changing nothing. There is no particular use for
words, read the commander a long time ago in a story
by a local writer. The story had stayed with him for
years, especially a scene in which the mother pricks
her finger with a needle and then explains something
to her daughter, and, in the end, the mother licks the
welling blood from her fingertip. The commander
winced: yes, he had been exposed to many deaths, both
day and night, but the needle prick to the fingertip
made all the deaths seem pointless. Meanwhile the

soldiers had come up to a twisted old fence that once probably served as a border crossing. In a whisper the commander cautioned them not to approach the fence and even ordered them to stand back. He huddled with Mladen and a corporal and they concurred: the fence was the last barrier and the enemy would have focused on it. No matter how hard they tried, however, the commander and his advisers could not agree on the next step. Dawn would soon be breaking, thought the commander, and he was at a dead end. A little later, in front of everyone, he whacked himself on the head and said now he understood. He spoke softly into the dark and sounded as if he'd never stop. In short, he explained he'd suddenly seen through the enemy's game. They'd figured the troops would assume the fence to be mined; he and his soldiers would be expected to detour around the fence and proceed, together, beyond it. Therefore, said the commander, we feel the fence itself won't be mined, but there will be pressure action mines planted alongside it on both sides to catch us when we go around it; the closer we stick to the middle section the safer we'll be. And as soon as he said this, the commander walked right up to it, threw his leg over the fence, and then, when nothing happened, called the others to follow. Alone or in pairs, the soldiers hopped over and soon it was behind them. The commander went back for a last look. He really wanted to toss a heavy rock sideways to set off one of the mines, but the blast would have given their location to the enemy. Better not, they thought, each of them, the commander and the soldiers. There are happy little moments like this of harmony, and everybody felt it. Far away before them the sky began to tear apart, and out of the crack gushed the bright, still sheepish, light of dawn. The commander summoned Mladen, told him to take another soldier and scout out what was going on around them. "You have ten minutes," said the commander, "because they'll see they've been hoodwinked, and they'll do their level best to find us." And so it was. First they heard shouts and random shots, then it was alternating bursts of gunfire and shell blasts. The checkpoint, thought the commander, has been obliterated. The shooting thumped a little longer, hand grenades blew and shells whistled, and then just as the shooting died down, everything reverberated with an explosion.

146

"Yes," whispered the commander, "oh, yes!" The magazine of weapons and munitions they'd left behind had just gone up, taking with it, hoped the commander, five or six enemy soldiers. Ah, the commander's thoughts continued, if someone had told me I'd in any way, at any time, and in any place actually desire a person's death, I'd never have believed them, but he was a soldier and he knew no one comes home unchanged from a war. It was good that he was surrounded by people in whom he had full confidence, at least he could trust them never to inform on him to the authorities or the police, though he always needed to be cautious, because if somebody reported him for having been earnestly sympathetic toward our alleged enemies, the commander would quickly find himself in a pickle. And even exile, whether forced or self-imposed, wouldn't save him. Had the weather been just a little more agreeable, he'd have gone, long ago, to a village by a shore. Which shore? we asked, the shore of a lake or the sea? Whatever, said the commander, whatever. We chose a boat. The weather was sunny and mild, no one was in a hurry, it was warm, July or August, we could hardly wait to stretch out and bask. The commander did a double take and saw he'd been left completely alone. He'd been asleep behind a bush, probably why they'd abandoned him. They have no idea, in fact, where I am, thought the commander, though they were all sure he'd be back. He always came back, so why not now? Then a gust of wind blew by and brought with it fragments of a commotion. The commander licked his finger and raised it into the air. Their fate, he thought, depends on which way the wind is blowing, and he set out in the direction it came from. He pushed his way through the bushes and came upon his soldiers, gathered around a hole in the ground; at the bottom there were sharpened spikes and on them were impaled three—three!—soldiers. The legs of one were still jerking and the soldiers were barely able to convince the commander that these were nothing but belated reflexes of the muscles and tendons, like a headless chicken lurching madly about the yard. They'd been walking down the road, they explained, and nothing hinted at the likelihood of a trap or threat. The pit was dug smack-dab in the middle, so sooner or later somebody would have fallen in. But who dug it and when? asked the commander. He'd have given anything for a proper answer, but apparently this was not sufficient. Some things are worth their weight, some their length, and some the degree to which they're absent. The more absent it is, the more costly a thing becomes—such a paradox. The commander finally realized that a buzzing sound he was hearing was coming from enemy soldiers who were streaming, in total disarray, down the slope and talking intensely, and the multitude sounded like the buzz of bees. The commander stepped back and cocked his head to the side, trying to stretch his field of vision to encompass all the participants. He tried to imagine his life elsewhere, but what reached him was the hum of the enemy's discontent, and he sought out Mladen: "If this continues," he said, "we're plunging straight into chaos." Their duty, the commander went on, was to settle on a secure route that would take him and the soldiers to safety. Mladen asked him, cautiously, how he knew which route was a good one. He didn't, said the commander, but he was absolutely certain he knew which of the routes was no good, so by the process of elimination it would be easy to ascertain which were viable, or at least had been viable at the outbreak of the conflict. What was expected of him? asked Mladen. The commander rubbed his chin and eyes, he was tired, terribly tired though he stood there and smiled, and it could be said that he wasn't present, or, perhaps, he was more present than ever, and he told Mladen to take two soldiers and lie in wait for the enemy riffraff that was obliterating everything as it passed through. The idea was for Mladen to fake a battle and keep moving to entice the enemy to follow him, not along the route their men were taking, but along another that splits off and leads across a ridge at some distance. On that path there were several huts and an old mill. A stream used to run in a torrent through there, especially in spring, and spin the water wheel, but then the stream dried up, leaving behind it a narrow ravine. If Mladen could lure them into the ravine, they wouldn't change direction until they'd realized their error, and by then it would already be night, or at least late evening, and this would allow the commander to cross the ridge at a much lower point, after which they'd have only a few miles left to the place where all units would assemble. Mladen nodded tersely and went off to find the soldiers. There weren't many left, and nobody, but nobody, was eager to accompany him. Mladen coaxed, pleaded, begged, made promises, but the soldiers had had it. "Somebody else can play," said one. The commander heard the words and was dismayed. Direct insubordination meant only one thing: a court martial and, probably, execution before a firing squad. The commander was overcome by an abrupt headache. He went over to the soldier who'd refused Mladen's summons and asked him whether he had any ibuprofen or aspirin. The soldier dipped a hand into a pocket and brought out a small white pill. "I wasn't asking for a sedative," said the commander. "If there's no proper medicine, any pill will do," said the soldier with a sudden grin. The commander shrugged, swallowed the white pill, and later, truth be told, he felt much better. He'd never learn whether it was the sedative or his immune system rebounding, but so it was with many things: there could be no talk or whining here: you took things as they were or you didn't take them at all. No negotiating or bargaining and wasting time on nonsense. This is life—thought the

commander, wrapped in the white veil of the sedative—not literature. As if confirming his words, shots
could be heard being fired somewhere behind his
back, exactly where Mladen was supposed to be drawing the enemy away onto the wrong route. "Aha,"
whispered the commander to himself. "If only we'd
had the time to dig a pit trap for them, they'd all be
in it now." But if there was anything they'd been short
of in this war, it was time, and when he gave it a little
more thought, the commander had to recognize that
the speed of events simply did not allow him to come
to a timely, fitting assessment, to weigh them in their
elemental and cosmic meaning, especially in the
cosmic, because there everything was pure, untainted
by malice and envy. The shots behind his back grew
sparser and soon they stopped altogether. There were
two or three spurts of gunfire, the sort usually used
to finish off the wounded and superfluous soldiers.
The commander trembled with a sudden bitter taste
in his mouth and hurried the troops. Some ten minutes later, however, they had to stop and wait for him
to vomit. He retched long and hard, his face drenched
in an icy sweat. His belly swelled and clenched though

it was already completely empty. He crouched by a beech tree and a soldier held his brow till the commander told him to stop. As soon as the soldier withdrew his hand, the commander sank to the ground next to the pool of vomit. As far as he was concerned, the war was over and he was prepared to lie there to the end of the world, but reality was something else and it compelled him to get up, so he summoned the strength and struggled to his feet as if he were rising, at the very least, from the dead. He stood there and stared at the soldiers standing before him: six soldiers, two corporals, and Mladen, who at that very moment stepped, blood-soaked, out of the brambles. "Where is my deputy?" asked the commander, but no one could say. He'd simply disappeared, period. No asking around would help and, besides, whom to ask? There is a misleading and heart-wrenching notion of war as the ideal time for forging friendships, rich with opportunities for self-sacrifice and dying for one's ideals, when, instead, these notions are all part of the farce that is war. War is a business like any other and these stories are merely a manifestation of efforts to consign the truth to oblivion, whence it will only be allowed to emerge once it conforms to the government's truth, but the honest truth would never accept that, and doesn't even now. "My dear soldiers," began the commander, but he stopped immediately because he felt tears welling. The commander, as is well known, had nothing against tears coursing down a man's cheeks, but he believed there are moments when one may cry in public, while crying at any other time would not do for men, and this moment was one when he was supposed to be spurring them all to finish their combat mission, to inspire them not to give up on life before their time, and one cannot do this with tears in one's eyes, right? The commander plucked a blade of grass and nibbled at it, sucking out its bitter sap, until the bitterness calmed him. "My dear soldiers, fellow combatants, brothers, the end of our part in yet another pointless war is upon us. We had no idea what we were fighting for, nor who our enemy was, and to be honest, we don't know what we'll find back home. I hope our houses are still standing, cozy and intact, like when we left them. The last stretch will probably be the most challenging: all the factions will be assembling here, and when faced with the absence of an enemy, troops often turn on one another. In any case, I wanted to warn you, whatever happens, do not break into song. There is always one of our number who doesn't appreciate that particular song and who will be out for revenge for no other reason." He stopped, he'd meant to say more but couldn't remember what. The soldiers applauded, and he ordered them to disperse. From afar they could hear the rumble of trucks and tanks that, apparently, had not bought into the pretense of Mladen's feigned combat, but guessing that he wanted to mislead them, had chosen the right path. "They'll be here any minute," repeated the commander, and Mladen, urging the remaining soldiers to disperse and get going uphill, along the route that would bring them home the fastest, as the commander had, apparently, announced in one of his earlier speeches when there were twice as many of them. They came over for a hug, but he shooed them off. "Once we make it home there will be time for that," he said, and brushed away a secret tear. It was time for him to go, the rumble of motors and caterpillar vehicles was so loud that he felt as if he were perched on a roof, waving a little flag with the coat of arms of some country during one of those big military parades. Up he shimmied into a tree. He climbed till he reached the densest part of the canopy, where nobody could possibly spot him, but he could still find the occasional gap between leaves to afford him at least a partial view of what was going on. He was surprised when he realized how vast a military force had been sent to chase down his handful of soldiers, as if liquidating his men was the primary objective of the military and civilian leaders. Hadn't the Nazis, once it had become clear that they were losing the war, proceeded with a panicked liquidation of the Jews, as if the outcome of the conflict depended only on that? In another, perhaps more courtly time, he would, by now, with full confidence, have sat down with the commander of the enemy troops and, over tea, or, why not, schnapps, traded anecdotes from their school days at the military academy, until they finally shook hands and congratulated each other on a well-earned victory or an amicable defeat. And each would then return tidily home to their impatient wives who, what with the long wait, had, probably, shown so much willingness to annex the new territories that everyone, in an odd way, was a little sorry the war was ending. Suddenly, right beneath the tree where the commander had, shall we say, nested, shouts went up. Through a gap in the leaves, the commander could see three of his soldiers. They were waving a piece of white cloth and walking slowly down the hill. When they reached the meadow they'd left only minutes before, on their way home, one of the tanks rolled toward them. Was it sniffing them? The gun barrel swiveled toward them, but then the tank kept rolling on. The soldiers, who hesitated longer than they should have, suddenly realized what the tank was up to, but by then it was too late and it rolled right over them, stopped, and reversed. The commander bit his hand to hold back the sobs and to stop himself from sliding down the tree, hot with the desire to give them what for. They'd kill him before he had the chance, of course, to pull a hand grenade from his boxers. He was left waiting and hoping there'd be people interested in a future project in which there'd be a role left for him to play the venerable gramps who'd been living in his coffin for years, but lovely Mistress Death wouldn't show her face. And then the enemy soldiers brought in their dogs. A dog loped right over to the tree where the commander was hiding, but nothing interested it beyond lifting a leg and spraying its mark; in a few days' time the mark would send a black bear scampering back to where it had come from because it wrongly assumed the scent was left by a grizzly (and it wasn't keen to run into a grizzly). The dogs raced off into the woods and soon their urgent barking could be heard, followed by gunshots and shouts. The commander was able to see the two corporals: the one covered in dog bites and gore was left to the dogs, while the other was sat down at a collapsible aluminum table and questioned quite calmly. And while the first corporal was dying in horrible agony, the other corporal sat cozily on a chair and responded with civility to the questions. They asked him for his name, what did he do, any brothers and sisters, how long had he been serving in the army, did he enjoy war, and other things to pass the time of day, his favorite writer, favorite actress, wife and kids, was his mother alive, and his father—was he retired, did he send him letters or postcards, and who were the smokers in his family? While he was answering, the corporal would occasionally gaze up into the treetop above, and at one moment, as he was staring at the mottled leaves, he was certain he'd seen someone's eye. He blinked and the eye was gone. This must be the eye of the Lord, and the corporal felt now God himself was looking after him. True, the eye reminded him of somebody, but of whom? As if through a fog the idea occurred to him that it was the commander perched in the treetop like a good-luck woodland sprite. Perhaps he might be able to climb up there once he'd finished with the questioning and pay him a visit. Then he told himself he was crazy, how could the commander be up in the tree, he was no owl hiding from the light of day, nor was he a songbird that had stopped chirping for a moment to peer down at a corporal who hadn't learned yet how to say "my death," but was studying hard and was a diligent student. And when, after some ten additional, courteous, and totally pointless questions, a knife flashed in the hand of the investigator, and he told the corporal he'd now be given his prize for his cooperative spirit. The corporal gave a slight smile, said he'd be glad to share his prize, threw himself with lightning speed on the investigator, wrested the knife free, and in what was almost a single move, slit the man's throat and in the same continuous sweep slit his own from ear to ear. The commander nearly found himself down there by the aluminum table, he was so wrapped up in the drama that had been playing out before him. Who knows, maybe he really was an owl and could see better in the dark than by the light of the sun? He'd wait for night to see; he wasn't going anywhere. He wondered how many of the soldiers were still alive, and he thought of Mladen and another two or three. And the cook? Really, where was the cook? Our cook is a fine cook, we all repeated, as if that fact—that the cook cooked well—was the standard response that included defense from any criminal proceedings that might have pertained to the cook, in uniform or civilian dress, regardless. But no one, not even the commander, could accuse the cook of a thing. There was that once, recalled the commander, when the hamburgers were not quite soft enough, but one doesn't go before a court for that, especially not a court martial. Beyond that, a few soldiers once criticized him for spending too much time in the kitchen, in the hot

seat and center of all life. The cook's answer was
simple: "I like listening to the radio," said the cook,
"and the reception is best there." This, regarding the
quality of the reception, was later confirmed by the
commander, who also liked to listen to the radio and
often went to the kitchen, he said, "for the good reception." He now cocked an ear, certain that among the
various planes and helicopters flying overhead he'd
be able to discern the sound of the motor of the plane
that was waiting for them at the airport in K. to bring
them to the capital city. We don't know whether there
is an international landing strip at K. but the toilets
in the parking lot by the airport are clean, cleaner
than many facilities in Europe and North America.
That must have been heard by some of the soldiers
who, below the commander's treetop, were at a loss
because toilets had suddenly become the main topic
of conversation and everywhere people were talking
only of them. And besides, if there were no more
soldiers to kill, let's at least talk about something
meaningful for all of us in war and peace. The conversation about toilets stirred the commander from
a precarious doze, and he didn't know whether to

laugh or cry. The doze was precarious because man is not a bird that can snooze on a wire or a branch, and he always feels as if he's sinking, dropping through whatever space he's in toward the very end of the world. Voices whispered things again to the commander, there's always someone who wants to be part of a secret alliance before all others, the more secretive the better, but then the commander had the impression he'd heard a familiar voice, he shifted silently and, sure enough, Mladen's voice. The commander wondered what miracle this could be, though he was perplexed, musing on what could have brought Mladen to the enemy's encampment. And then everything halted, transformed, and we were left alone as we'd never been before, because everything took on a different meaning, and the world became a backward mirror in which nothing was as it was, but as it might be. The commander looked into the mirror and saw himself tiny as a frog. He'd have been happiest stomping on himself, thought the commander, and he relished the scene of the actual act of dispersal, the heart flying off to the right, the liver to the left, the brain straight up, aspiring—in vain, of course—to celestial heights. The brain can ultimately be deep-fried; that is, probably, the only thing it is useful for. And what else, thought the commander, when it hadn't warned him in time of what, even without his brain, he should have seen: that Mladen had been playing a double game the whole time, and he was, in fact, a spy for the enemy. Everything abruptly assumed an altered aspect, what had been unclear became clear, the inexplicable could be explained, and comprehension replaced incomprehension. All of Mladen's undertakings, his triumphant arrivals after finishing his tasks, the conversations when he'd asked detailed questions about the commander's plans and intentions, the ease with which he insisted there was no point to investigating the whole passel of murders of soldiers around the checkpoint, all this now suggested a different story, a story in which Mladen played the leading role, including the most sinister role, the role of merciless executioner. The commander had known, of course, that a different explanation was also possible, one by which Mladen had been compelled to obey commands from the highest military authority to convince the enemy of his loyalty. This would be easy for the commander to test. All he had to do was jump down and see what Mladen would do then, if he'd kill him or protect him in some way. But why should he, thought the commander, something should be left for the historians, those parasites who shape history whichever way they like, they who were themselves never part of history. Something had started happening down below, the soldiers were preparing to move, but first, as the commander could see, they were laying mines along the path that led upward, toward home. Several mines they planted around a nearby stream as well, and there would be woodland creatures killed by them that very night; the next morning the stream would be littered with the body parts of the animals. The people would be killed later. Not daring, still, to come down from the tree, the commander again fell asleep in his treetop and missed seeing the arrival of what must have been his last two soldiers, and hence he was unable to stop them from treading on the mines. The commander started from a dream in which he'd been eating a cheese burek, and for a moment he didn't know what was happening. Then he understood, but first he thought of Mladen. He'd find Mladen a little later, along the path the enemy soldiers and tanks had gone. They hadn't taken him with them for long, and besides now this was one less mouth to feed, and that seemed most important just then. The commander leaned over and rifled through Mladen's jacket pockets. Apparently someone had already done the same before him, because, aside from an old bus ticket and a few coins, he found nothing. Then he remembered to check the pants pockets and there he found a black booklet in which Mladen had entered all his meetings and contacts with the other side. For us, this was a bonanza, it was nothing short of a list of the people who had worked to disappear us from the face of the earth. In the end they'd have all fared as Mladen did, this was the gruesome truth and nobody could fathom their willingness to do something that ultimately brought with it only loss. He continued searching Mladen's corpse, and came across a thicker place on the right front side below his belt. He started unbuckling the belt but heard voices approaching and quickly dipped into the woods. While he was waiting for the voices to move off, he mused how he could have cashed his chips in with such a lack of caution, and then back he quietly went to where Mladen's body lay—the body was gone. "Who could have taken it?" asked the commander softly, though he knew there was nobody around who could answer. Such things happened elsewhere, didn't they? If they did, then they did, and there's no cause for concern. He circled some twenty paces in both directions, but nowhere did he see footprints. He probably hadn't looked carefully enough or hadn't counted his paces well, but when he turned, prepared to head home, he saw two soldiers carrying Mladen's lifeless body. He didn't know who was more surprised, the enemy soldiers or our commander, but he collected himself quicker and with lightning speed (though to observers on the sidelines, had there been any, it would have looked incomparably slower) he aimed his weapon at them. The soldiers simultaneously threw their hands up, and Mladen's body plunked down onto the path. "Watch out!" shouted the commander. "That's not scrap iron to be thrown around like that." The soldiers looked at each other and then one said, "But he's dead, sir, nothing more can happen to him." The commander wagged a finger: "You can never be sure of that, soldier. Miracles might happen at any moment. But first tell me: how did you learn my language?" The soldier laughed: "Your language? This is my language!" The commander nodded, pensive, then suddenly stared at the soldier. "My, my, are you one of the Dejanovićes?" asked the commander and when the soldier said he was, the commander asked, "What are you after here? Hands down and scram, you and your buddy." The soldiers dropped their hands and trudged slowly downhill, but the soldier Dejanović stopped and asked, "And you? What are you after here?" The commander said nothing for a time, then pointed his gun at them and barked, "Want to see what I'm after, really?" He aimed a short burst of gunfire above their heads and, bumping each other, they sprinted away. The commander waited for them to move beyond some bushes and then he went back to Mladen's body. He saw his belt and pants were unbuckled and he knew that whatever was hidden there had been forever lost. He should have frisked the soldiers. And now he had to worry about a new posse of the enemy that would be organized as soon as the two of them reached the meadow. He should have killed them then and there instead of inquiring about their language. One speaks the language one speaks and everyone will always speak the language they speak, and the language of the victors will always be on top, and so it goes. Besides, it would be funny if the victor were to speak the language of the loser, just as it was entirely natural for the loser to speak the language of the victor. But what about when the victor and loser speak the same language? What then? The commander didn't like these writerly tricks that threw him into doubt and required of him at least a measure of wisdom, but still he tried to wriggle free of the trap and said, "Then, quick, think up a new language. That, at least, is easy!" Nothing is easy, thought the commander, but for language, at least, this couldn't be easier. All I need is a little persistence and everyone will accept what is foisted on them. "Language is habit," whispered Mladen softly as if to himself, but with a ring of triumph. "Repeat a word or phrase long enough, and you'll end up thinking you came up with it yourself. And when you think you've created a word, you can allow yourself to feel that you created the world." The commander couldn't believe his ears: the body they'd all thought to be dead was now talking, and it showed no intention of stopping! He went over to it again and at that very moment Mladen's eyes popped open, he sat up, and looked around. "Nice," he said, "nobody's here. The whole area is only ours, yours and mine, or, if you prefer, yours *or* mine. A big difference for such a small word, eh?" He squinted slyly, which he'd never done before and which sent our commander into shivers. But nothing could be predicted here, though the commander did think the time was nigh for a final reckoning, and, indeed, this swiftly led to further developments. Mladen had risen to his feet, made an effort to tidy up his uniform and put himself in order, and then from an embroidered sheath he pulled out a long, gleaming knife. With a bent finger he beckoned to the commander to come over. "What's this," wondered the commander, "a horror rerun of the events that played out just now, or a real game of fate that could turn a vegetarian into a meat-eater and then promote the meat-eater to a cannibal?" All these, he knew, might merely be symbols, pretense, empty lies and promises, nothing had to be substantial, obligating, genuine. But Mladen was brandishing a real knife with a sharp blade and there could be no doubt that the wounds inflicted by the cold steel would be every bit as real. The commander, however, did not have a knife; he had only a small spade he'd forgotten to take off his belt, so he pulled it out and with it rebuffed Mladen's first attack. All the while he was trying to remember what this whole event reminded him of, and he finally realized it was one of those mixed-genre movies where for the first half they develop into something like a police procedural, and then, when a clock at some point strikes midnight, everything shifts to a saga about vampires and an assortment of living dead. He'd rather have tossed away the spade that, panting, he was holding out in front of him, but then Mladen would have to put down his knife first or slip it back into the embroidered sheath, and he showed no inclination to do so. Instead he began moving slowly toward the people who were waiting in line to buy tickets for the New World. "New Belgrade?" asked the man at the bus station counter and the commander had to gently but confidently repeat: "The New World." "I don't see much difference there," said the man and lowered the curtain. "And what now?" asked the commander, and Mladen said, "Now we fight." And with a wild shriek he threw himself at the commander. The people who had been waiting peacefully in line scattered with shouts and curses, and the commander and Mladen stopped to let them pass. The commander did not stop to ask where this line of people who were waiting to buy bus tickets in the middle of the forest had come from, with not a single bus route in sight. "Well, there you're wrong," barked Mladen and threw himself, again, like a wild beast at the commander, who had more luck than smarts. For a moment he was distracted, and it could have cost him his life. Instead it was just his shirt that suffered. Mladen aimed his knife well but the loose, blousy shirt threw off his calculations and, at the same time, saved the commander's life. The commander shook his head to free himself of unwanted thoughts about buses for New Belgrade or the New World, whichever. The miss threw Mladen off-kilter, and for a moment, when his knife fell from his hand, he found himself in a completely hopeless fix, the whiteness of his neck even flashed as if summoning or answering the gleam of the knife. "Now!" the commander heard a loud and unfamiliar, clear voice. "Now's the time to grab the knife. Next time will be too late." "And maybe there won't be a next time," added yet another voice, much softer than the first. The commander stared at his hand and then at the hands of his opponent. The opponent was gradually recovering his balance, this could be seen by his focus, his furrowed brow, the tip of his tongue between his lips. And the commander raised the knife and lowered it, raised it and lowered it, and went on raising and lowering it until he felt it plunge into something solid, something tangible, something that bled. Everyone seated around the table had bloodied lips and many drops of blood on their cheeks, collars, cuffs, pants. Meanwhile Mladen was dying, bereft of any hope of surviving such an attack and so many stabs and wounds around his head. He lay on his side, coughed and spit blood, and, all in all, felt decidedly under the weather. He thought he'd appreciate the opportunity of holding a farewell speech, but the growling of the dogs warned him that, with their change of owner they'd changed appetites, and, shuddering, he sighed once more and soon after that felt his life ebb and that instant he, Mladen, was officially dead. "I'm not sorry," thought Mladen with his last prickles of consciousness, he'd lived a pleasant life, traveled the world and . . . and . . . that was it, that's called death. "So, kids," said the commander, "you see why you shouldn't succumb to crime, drugs, unprotected sex, and unlimited time in front of the television. Moderation and modesty are the two essential virtues, and it's enough to hold to them; they'll replace all others . . . ." In the end it always turns out that the commanding officers are safe while they send the rank and file—the young who still haven't inhaled the aroma of life—to the sacrificial altar. Out of the corner of his eye, the commander could see Mladen's body jerking and was seized by terror at the thought that the agony might not be over. Mladen's eyes were still open and the commander tried shutting them, but no matter how hard he struggled he couldn't, even with the help of members of the blues group Fruity Juice, who suddenly appeared on the path, going from house to house, though nobody asked them anything, offering services, church almanacs, and wooden spoons. The hippie attire of the members of the group and the kerchiefs over their frightful shaggy heads of hair couldn't dupe the commander, who was certain they were Jehovah's Witnesses in disguise. All this meant that the commander was no longer at all sure, to put it mildly, of where he was. If he was still on the path, why didn't a single driver take an interest, why didn't they ask what this young man was doing here, and if he was waiting, for whom? And where was the posse? Did the dogs get it wrong and lead them off elsewhere? And then an awful thought occurred to him: what if they were already right here, standing close by, hidden by the bushes? The dogs, of course, would be shushed, waiting only for the commander to finish his story and then they'd attack. But the commander didn't wait. He bent over, pretending to fiddle with his shoelaces, and he only used this as a pretense to inch over to an automatic weapon lying on the ground. He made as if to straighten up, then flung himself down, snatched up the gun and began shooting in all directions. While shooting, he rolled over to the right toward the path's edge and from there scurried on all fours into deeper underbrush. Behind him, on the path where Mladen's body lay, staggered wounded soldiers, some dropped dead and others cursed. He shoved his hand into his pocket and pulled out a fistful of capsules marked with a skull and cross-bones. This was dog poison, and he strewed it around on the path over Mladen's body, to take effect imme-diately. Sure enough, soon he could hear a dog whim-per, then another, then a third, and all three wailed together a little longer until an uncomfortable silence took over. Now he could move on, thought the com-mander, and, crouching close to the ground, he crawled toward an opening in the shrubs. In order to make himself even smaller and less visible, he imag-ined himself a worm or a slug and squirmed among the brambles and twigs. Reaching the end of the thicket, he saw a great meadow, a slope thick with grass and other greenery, which at first glance looked like a rug carpeting a room from wall to wall. However, soon it became clear that this was an illusion; his feet sank into the dense grass or slid over it, especially where the slope was steeper. Luckily, what was imped-ing his progress did the same for the men who were after him, except that in their efforts to be as speedy as possible they tripped with each step and tumbled down the hill. They were at the foot of the slope just as the commander had nearly scrambled to the top, or, actually, not far from a spot where the grassy slope became a rocky ridge; on its other side—the same place the path with the land mines had led to—would bring him to a border crossing and safe return home. Slipping, but this time on rocks skittering out from under his feet, the commander thought about how he'd set out with many, but now here he was returning alone. "I am Odysseus," he sobbed bitterly, but he soon stopped mainly because he was no longer sure whether Odysseus came back alone or with a few surviving warriors, and besides, unlike Odysseus, he, the commander, had nobody waiting for him at home. Just then, the commander thought of the cook. Whatever happened to the cook? Only moments later the commander came across a gruesome sight: a dozen large birds crouching on a carcass, ripping off chunks of flesh with their hooked beaks. The commander thought, a mountain goat, but only when he came closer and shooed away the greedy raptors did he realize that before him lay the half-gnawed body of the company's cook. He recognized the man by his large head and one pale blue eye—the other eye had been devoured along with the tongue and a part of the cheek. While he was inspecting the cook, the commander felt a wave of nausea, staggered over to the nearest rock and heaved, whimpering like the dogs who'd been poisoned a bit ago. Who knows, maybe he'd ingested a little poison while scattering the capsules around Mladen's corpse. From childhood he'd had the habit of licking his fingers after everything he did, regardless of whether he was laying heads of cabbage in a sauerkraut barrel, or feeling through a fish fillet for the treacherous bones, or sprinkling salt on food, or adding the sugar to the cream filling when baking pastry. He'd always lick at least one finger, regardless of whether he'd actually touched something with it, so he'd probably done the same after scattering the capsules. What an idiot I am, muttered the commander, and went ahead lambasting himself with choice curses. Though he'd already retched, his belly was still distended and aching; he shoved two fingers down his throat to empty his stomach. The new wave left him gasping, and he thought his end had truly come. His gut tightened and stretched in attempts to separate the good from the bad, but he knew it was a lost cause that would only end when his stomach was completely empty. As he was gagging, the scavengers began to move freely around him. The commander felt a moist fog had settled over him; he kept having to squint and wipe away the sweat from his brow and cheeks. He could no longer stand, his legs were wobbling, so he dropped to his knees and found himself eye to eye with the cook's remains. Maybe, he thought, he was destined to meet his end while guarding the hollowed remnants of the cook. He peered down the slope but didn't see anyone. Again he was nudged by a presentiment that the enemy was at hand, watching him and sneering and waiting for his attention to flag, and when it flagged they'd rush in and snatch him along with the other prisoners, as if preparing for their triumphal return to Rome. The commander winced, crossed himself sneakily, and began collecting his belongings. He couldn't find the key to his apartment but breathed a sigh of relief when he remembered he'd left it in the pocket of his other pants—stuffed into his pack, as were all his other clothes, his shorts, socks, underpants, handkerchiefs. He remembered how he'd packed while he was readying to leave with the company for the new combat situation, and it seemed that six months had passed since then, perhaps even eight, though everything had, in fact, happened over some fifteen days, three weeks, a month, maybe, no more, for sure, absolutely sure, which would mean that he must have at least twenty-one daily reports in his ledger, maybe twenty-five pages of notes, which would be easy to check by leafing through the ledger, but it was at the bottom of his pack under the dirty laundry, out of reach, especially now when at any moment the company would start to march. The commander knocked his head, yet again he'd forgotten there was no more company, he was alone. He looked at the sky and saw the sun had begun to set, it was squeezing the tube from which night would squirt, and under the cover of dark the commander would trek across the last miles separating him from home. At first this seemed the most challenging stretch of the whole journey, especially because the passage would transport him through the border of another country, across terrain that yawned open wide, which the soldiers had to traverse as speedily as possible, hoping to dodge enemy bullets. But now the commander was alone and he couldn't decide whether this heightened his chances, or, possibly, diminished them. Diminished probably: when fewer were crossing, the gunfire would be focused on each soldier. So if the commander dared to dash across the unsheltered ground on his own, he could count on all the officials at the border post training their weapons on him. He wasn't overly concerned, he was still confident that his lucky star shielded him as it had so far. He tossed his pack onto his back, darted a glance at the slope and again thought back to their arrival. He saw himself at the head of the company, talking cheerfully as they approached the spot where they'd been assigned to operate the checkpoint that had been held by their allies. Everything else, admitted the commander, was an improvised and endless frustration. Who needed the checkpoint, and what was it checking? When he'd asked that question of the colonel who delivered the order that had come from the Supreme Staff, the colonel replied that such things would be dealt with in stride. Ultimately, said the colonel, the checkpoint is a two-way street, somebody is always crossing from one side to the other, meaning, added the colonel, that there would always be work for those charged with its maintenance. But, the commander dared interject, does that mean our position in the conflict will change, or that we'll turn our backs on old alliances and form new ones? The colonel's face fell, and he said the commander couldn't have heard any such thing from him. He, meaning the colonel, had merely served as a bearer of tidings, a courier, a screw in an intricate mechanism, no more. If the colonel was nothing but a screw, thought the commander, then what could he—meaning the commander—say for himself? He wasn't a screw or even a tack, smaller yet, or as thin as a straight pin, coming back—as he was— alone, without a single soldier, without even a cook. He did quickly make a point of saying that the story of the cook was a mesmerizing one, so he'd leave it for better times, because the cook's heroism, he said, definitely deserved that. But first of all the commander thought he'd go to the military archive and investigate what had transpired with the various alliance treaties and protocols for collaboration; this might be the only way to explain the fact that his unit, obliged to hold the only checkpoint in the vicinity and beyond, had always been in the crosshairs of the opposing forces, even when the current opponents had until very recently been allies. And while he mused over the last few weeks, the thought kept bothering him that, without his knowledge, of course, the whole company had been a part of a cruel experiment, and they were sacrificed so insights on the structure of warfare could be gathered, which, in other words, meant that no one was to blame for what happened to the soldiers and commander. A cruel thought, thought the commander, but not implausible. Cruelty is, alas, sometimes necessary for the pursuit of the proper path toward tenderness, but in his unit's case no one had given two cents for tenderness, instead an army bureaucrat had had the bright idea that the time was ripe for a study of the impact on soldiers of a sudden shift in the enemy's standing (in other words when friend becomes foe, or vice versa). What happened presumed not a reality-based result—the outcome of earlier events in this same reality—but instead a faux reality, a strategy game like Battleship, always in barter mode, always opening with "What if . . .", which would not, in and of itself, have attracted such attention, especially in comparison to the media frenzy when pop and rock stars breeze through an army center or R & R site. But to experiment with real people, to measure and chalk up points for the corpses of the ones who had had a shortage of luck, or maybe, instead, had a surplus, was something else again, though it essentially came down to the same thing. "Had" and "had not" were, at least in this situation, largely interchangeable and the only thing to keep an eye out for, in the spirit of stylistic purity, was to avoid using them three or four times per sentence. And it mattered less whether the sentence pertained to customs inspection, or to searches for new books and narrative voices. Of course, there were sentences for which there was nothing to be done so they stayed as they were, such as: "We had to add two more soldiers, but this changed nothing. They only succeeded in postponing the inevitable. Of course, we hadn't considered the dogs, because we still hadn't succeeded in laying the appropriate path, and at first, when we heard the dogs, we thought of sheep that bleat and move with their flock, but later, when we saw the effect the dogs had and learned that the percentage of waste had been minimal (as long as the time for understanding the stories was prolonged), we felt we were able to and dared to continue." The commander clutched his head, hoping the pain would wake him, but he felt no pain, everything was dull and shimmering like light shining through mist. Then the cook, again, popped into his mind. How had the cook made it this far before all the rest of them, how had he clambered up the hillside, and how had he even known that this was the place to cross over, and, by that same token, that there was, probably, a tunnel under the river, and that there was lateral drainage, all of this being information that he, the commander, had been given in a file marked in red with the English words TOP SECRET written across it, which, by the way, always irritated him, because he could not understand why these words were used and not others such as SECRET OF SECRETS, well maybe not, or, simply NAJVIŠA TAJNA in Serbian. Whatever the case, he had decided to accept the offer and lead the hand-picked company at the checkpoint. As we've said, the checkpoint was hardly a new building, it had been in use for many years with sleeping quarters, lecture hall, mess hall, the pantry and the commander's small room. The small room was small indeed, but suited him fine. The only thing that bothered him was the lack of an en suite bath and toilet, but the soldiers kept the shared latrine tidy, and the commander often went there to enjoy the fresh fragrance of the air freshener. The commander might have seemed to be overdoing things just a wee bit with his upbeat description, sounding more like an ad for the sale of vacation cottages, but we knew this was not the case. The commander really did like the checkpoint, and he felt it was a place he could live, of course not during war, but during peace. Here he could breathe deeply, surrounded by forests full of conifers, and everything would be calm, slow, as if its weight had been jettisoned and it was prepared at any moment for takeoff. To see all of this from above, thought the commander, what a thrill that would be! He imagined a scene in which geometry played the lead, turning the forest into an elongated rectangle, the meadows into a multi-colored chessboard, the hills into cones, and the river into a curving line that yearned to be straight. Yes, thought the commander, some wishes are never fulfilled. He'd said the same the first or second evening after arriving at the checkpoint. The evening was divine, the sky full of stars, the soldiers tired from travel and quartered in the building, and in front of it crackled a fire, a little fire of dry grass, twigs, and an assortment of leaves. A step or two from the fire began the dark, and the commander at one moment said he had always dreamed of leaving the world of light for the world of the dark, but never had had the courage to try. A soldier lazily lifted his head and asked him why he didn't do it then; all it would take were a few steps. And to have the resolve, of course, someone added, to never come back. The commander tried to defend himself, but the soldiers were unforgiving, they chanted, helped him stand and pointed him toward the fire. They left him when they felt too much heat. The commander, alone, took two more small steps, then one longer one, stepping over the flames, and then on he walked until he was certain he had completely sunk into the darkness. He turned and, clearly, as if under a magnifying glass, saw the soldiers staring tensely into the dark, and then he realized he could easily decide to never go back. True, none of us had ever been sure what such a decision would mean and whether pursuing that route was even possible. By no means did we want anybody to think we'd imposed a different choice on him. He himself chose it, so he did, and he was, himself, responsible in full for everything that would happen with it and to him. From the dark it was he, after all, who stepped into the light and then it became clear that he'd been fighting sincerely against the darkness that had been hampering and refusing to release him. And who knows what would have happened here if one of the soldiers hadn't charged with his bayonet and hacked through all the finer and coarser filaments of darkness, which had latched like leeches to the commander's back, arms, and legs. And when the bayonet slashed through them, we could all hear the darkness bleat in pain, but that, we cried, is something like the song of the sirens with which they hoped to lure Odysseus, and if someone responds to the song, that person will never again see the light of day. This is why we all spun around as fast as greased lightning, and plugged the commander's ears. The words "We won't relinquish our Odysseus" buzzed among the soldiers, and this surge of a feeling of unity brought tears to many eyes. The commander had to admit he hadn't in years met such a feeling of camaraderie and understanding and this made all the more painful what happened on that miserable hillside path that led *to* the checkpoint and *from* the checkpoint, all depending on which side of the barrier a person was standing and in which direction he was looking. The commander sniffled and gazed around with tearful eyes. What actually happened, did anything happen, and might it happen again—to all these questions the commander had no real answer. And besides, so many unresolved questions pressed in on him that he could barely walk. It could even be said that he didn't walk but waddled like a duck. That reminded him of the Peking duck that the company cook had prepared once, the most delicious thing the commander had ever tasted. It was difficult for him to reconcile the image of the roast duck with the sight of the corpse among the rocks at the top of the slope. The corpse looked as if it had never accomplished a

thing in its lifetime, and the commander then thought
of the other young dead, the sorrow that spread
unstoppably from them in all directions, becoming
ever more cumbersome with each death, until no one
could budge it. And so it lay there like a transparent
resin or a scum on the face of the world, resisting the
solving of the mystery. But there can be no mystery
that cannot be solved, felt the commander, and he
refused to step off the path of the transport of sorrow.
He stood there motionless, holding a STOP! sign up
in the air, thinking he was in the right place, and then,
when he'd only barely dodged the frenzied vehicles of
sorrow, he realized the times had still not changed.
Everybody was still thinking in well-trodden categories that reliably (as they saw it) divided the world
into plus and minus, light and dark, male and female,
leaving no place whatsoever for all those who, delib-
erately or otherwise, stepped out of the black-and-
white picture and did what they could to free up some
small space, the seats of future change, which would
slowly grow until they took their place in the new
world. A new world, thought the commander, and
that same moment he remembered how much

goodwill and readiness his soldiers had brought to fixing up the checkpoint, how they scrubbed everything several times over, as the grime had soaked so deeply into the grain of all things, until each object shone as if it were new. And later they sat in the dark and munched on the fruit they'd picked that day in an orchard that they'd happened upon by chance while they were on their way to the checkpoint. The gate to the orchard was open as if enticing them in, and they happily threw themselves into picking the fruit. There were apples to be had, and apricots, pears, peaches, and plums. While the soldiers picked the fruit, at first stealthily and then louder, the commander went on to the bottom of the orchard, curious about why there seemed to be no proprietor in sight. The orchard was vast, as if it had no end, and the commander was about to give up when he finally spotted the cottage where the orchard guard or owner presumably lived. The outer door was ajar, as was the inner door, and the commander suddenly felt his heart pound, his fingers clutched his pistol tighter, his mouth grew unbearably dry. The commander knew what this was: his body's danger reflex, but what sort of danger could there be among the fruit trees? Nevertheless he pulled out his pistol, bent over, and studied the windows. From a great distance the voices of the soldiers wafted his way, no louder than the buzzing of bees. The commander realized he ought to have brought with him at least one other soldier, to meet the security minimum, too late now. He determined the angle along which he should approach the cottage without being spotted from the windows, and step by step, slowly, quietly, he reached the front door. By the doorway, in a pool of blood, lay a middle-aged man. His mouth was slightly agape, he looked as if he'd died from the strain of singing, but in fact somebody had slit his throat ear to ear. The commander stepped carefully over the murdered man, and then he heard a woman's unintelligible voice coming from the lower part of the cottage, the cellar, or ground floor. The commander noticed a set of cement stairs leading to the lower area, and he slowly started down. The garbled voices began to take shape, and he could already tell that the voices were of two men and a woman. The men were saying something, even laughing, while the woman's voice only moaned. There was another woman, however, in the room, as the commander later saw, but she was opening her mouth in vain, and made no sound at all. One of the men was holding her and slapping her each time she tried to shut her eyes or turn her head away. "Look," said the man each time. "Look, when I tell you, look and learn!" And what she was supposed to be watching was a little girl, about ten, clearly her daughter, who was being raped by the other man, panting and dripping with sweat. Both of them were soldiers, but the commander couldn't recognize the uniforms, the more so because of the drips of sweat pouring into his eyes. His recognition would have changed nothing. Their actions would have been the same. First he stepped softly into the room, rested the pistol on the head of the soldier who was raping the little girl, signaled to the other to shut up, then, without a word, he pulled the trigger, and while the soldier crumpled to the floor, he put his gun to the head of the other soldier, told the woman to close her eyes, and fired a second shot. The soldier slithered down the wall and pulled the woman down with him. The woman's voice suddenly returned, and she began screaming with all her might. She crawled over to the other end of the room where her bloodied daughter lay. The child shuddered and pulled away from the woman's touch, and only then did she squirm free of the soldier's legs, lying across hers like paperweights. The commander tore his gaze from the woman and girl, turned, and went back to the orchard. He didn't say a word to the others, but urged the soldiers to finish picking fruit and continue on their way toward the checkpoint. The daily routine at the checkpoint, however, and the accelerated pace with which things began to happen, helped other things to be forgotten, especially the things that happened when they were on their way there. And so the commander stopped and thought back as if he'd been away for twenty years and not just a month, plus or minus a day. He took one more glance at the half-gnawed body of the cook and then, following signs that only he could see, he bent over to touch a rock at the beginning of a narrow path. If this was the real path, he'd be able to feel three hollows. There they were, three, and the commander stood up, took three more steps of differing lengths, closed his eyes and turned around in a circle, and when he opened his eyes again he was in front of a light-blue door. He turned the handle and strode into the apartment. He walked around it, peered into each room, the bathroom, and the front hall. Everything was just as he'd left it, though it was actually all different. He washed his hands in the kitchen and looked for cookies. He could tell that he reeked of grime and sweat, but that, he decided, could wait. Into the living room he went, picked up the television remote and sat in an armchair. He clicked it on, the television began to hum, and the commander saw himself there on the screen. "How did I get here?" asked the commander. "How?" smiled the female talk-show host. "Here's how," she said, "we make every effort to keep close to our viewers and fulfill their most varied wishes." The commander smiled, "Don't tell me someone wished to see me." He turned his face to the ceiling and loudly sniffed the air. The talk-show host asked him, concerned, if everything was all right. "Naturally," answered the commander, and explained that he was sniffing to establish whether there were any enemies in the vicinity. "Do tell," said the talk-show host. "You sniff them out, do you?" The commander looked at her: the talk-show host was wearing the shortest skirt and had the longest legs he had ever seen. "They," said the commander, "have a different smell than we do." The host twiddled a lock of hair, and said, "It must be they don't bathe." "No," agreed the commander, "they never bathe and seldom use deodorant." The talk-show host was about to say something, but she was interrupted by a voice from the crew. "We had a brief interruption, so we'll run that again, ten seconds! Ready? Okay? Now!" The talk-show host licked her lips and said, "Our mystery guest today has just returned from combat. This is not your first war, is it? What has made this war different from all other wars?" The commander also licked his lips, frowned, and, with a pensive voice, said: "Oh, so many things. For instance the previous war was frontal, major and enduring battles were led with the deployment of armored units and aviation. This one now is much smaller and largely fought by guerilla groups, meaning it is much less expensive and less spectacular and compelling for the media." The talk-show host glanced at a slip of paper shaking in her hand: "And here we already have a question from one of our viewers . . . . She would like to know whether soldiers curse a lot, and if they do curse, and she has heard them curse, what does the commander do about it?" The commander squirmed in the leather armchair, wiped the sweat from his forehead, remembering halfway through the gesture that he'd been told not to brush away his sweat because he'd smudge the powder they'd used on his face. "He doesn't do anything," said the commander, "because the young woman who asks would curse, too, if she herself were there." The talk-show host laughed: "She's no young woman, she's fully grown. She's my mother." The commander tried to muster a smile to match her smile, but his upper lip had already pooled so much sweat that a little stream of it was dribbling off his chin; with broad sweeps he dabbed two spots while the director's assistant scowled at him and shook her head. "And my last question," announced the talk-show host, "did anything nice happen to you in this war?" The commander thought for a moment and then said, "I survived." The talk-show host looked at him: "That's it?" "That's it," repeated the commander, and he felt so awkward for a moment that he wanted to slap himself. But he managed to calm down, waited for the credits to scroll by, and meanwhile chatted with the talk-show host, staring freely at the shadow under her skirt until she uncrossed her legs. Then he got up and went to the bathroom, where he bashed himself with all his strength on the nose. The blow was painful, much more so than the commander had expected, his nose even changed shape and swelled right up, and blood ran from both nostrils. While stanching the flow with tissues and cold compresses, he remembered the cook and thought he should have covered the body with rocks and not abandoned him to the whims of the vultures. He felt a huge wave of exhaustion and he barely resisted the urge to lie down that instant, where he happened to be standing. He first went to the front door, turned the lock twice, and hooked the chain. A little additional security was never remiss. After all, there was a war on.

ABOUT THE AUTHOR

"A Kafka for our times" (*Neue Zürcher Zeitung*), DAVID ALBAHARI was born 1948 in Péc, Serbia. He studied English language and literature in Belgrade. In 1994 he moved to Calgary, Canada with his wife and their two children, where he still lives today. He mainly writes novels and short stories and is also an established translator from English into Serbian. He is a member of the Serbian Academy of Sciences and Arts. His collection of short stories, *Description of Death*, won the Ivo Andrić Award for the best collection of short stories published in Yugoslavia in 1982 and his novel *Bait* the NIN Award for the best novel published in Yugoslavia in 1996. His latest collection of stories, *Every Night in Another Town*, has won the important Vital Award, one of the most significant literary awards in Serbia. His books have been translated into sixteen languages. English translations include a selection of short stories, entitled *Words*

Are Something Else, as well as four novels: *Tsing*, *Bait*, *Snow Man*, and *Götz and Meyer*. He has translated into Serbian many books by authors such as Saul Bellow, Isaac Bashevis Singer, Thomas Pynchon, Margaret Atwood, V. S. Naipaul, and Vladimir Nabokov as well as plays by Sam Shepard, Sarah Kane, Caryl Churchill, and Jason Sherman. He was a participant in the International Writing Program in Iowa (1986) and International Writer-in-Residence at the University of Calgary, under the auspices of the Markin-Flanagan Distinguished Writers Program (1994–95). Between 1991 and 1994 he was president of the Federation of Jewish Communities in Yugoslavia.

ABOUT THE TRANSLATOR

ELLEN ELIAS-BURSAĆ has been translating fiction and non-fiction by Bosnian, Croatian, and Serbian writers since the 1980s. The AATSEEL Award for Best Translation into English was given to her translation of David Albahari's short-story collection *Words Are Something Else*, and ALTA's National Translation Award was given to her translation of Albahari's novel *Götz and Meyer* in 2006. Her book *Translating Evidence and Interpreting Testimony at a War Crimes Tribunal: Working in a Tug-of-War* was given the Mary Zirin Prize in 2015.